GLIMPSES OF INFINITY

A Write Minds
Anthology

This anthology is published by
Inside Out Community
The Eastern Angles Centre
Gatacre Road
Ipswich
Suffolk
IP1 2LQ

First published 2021

Thanks to the Lottery Community Fund for their support with this project.

Typesetting by Alan Vickers in Times New Roman and Futura

Cover Photo: Green Wind (2006) by Diane Maclean.
At the Tump, Ravenswood, Ipswich.
Green Wind is a wind-reactive sculpture with wings made of coloured stainless steel that turn 360° in the wind. The colour is created by an oxide layer on the polished surface of the material that reacts with daylight to create colour change. The sculpture changes colour with the seasons and the times of the day. The height of the columns varies from 7-10 metres.

Contents

Black river
That wends its way through this town
Lies forgotten.

Introduction

Petra McQueen

Teaching is always a privilege but being part of Write Minds has been particularly special. Students come from all walks of life and can, therefore, write with insight about subjects and places that are alien to me. We have former homeless people and former headteachers; cooks and computer analysts; scientists and artists. Each person brings their unique vision and voice to the classes. The only thing our students truly have in common is that they have struggled with their mental health at some point. No one dwells on this though as we are all too busy discussing literature and writing. At Inside Out Community, the arts in mental health charity that runs Write Minds, the underlying assumption is that being creative – either through art, music, dance or, in our case, creative writing – is not only fun but will allow people space away from their difficulties. It may also allow students to process traumatic events in a safe supportive environment.

There is high level of respect and kindness within the group which means that people feel free to share their writing and to experiment with it. When I think about the atmosphere produced by the students, I see it as a safe white space into which each student can enter and feel respected and heard. I was afraid that with the necessary introduction of Zoom recently, the safe space would be lost – thankfully, experience has proved me wrong. Although we are coming from twelve different homes across four counties, the safe space remains. In consequence there is an honesty about our students' work which is found in the best of writing.

Each week for the last seven years or so, I have set a writing task in class and some homework outside of class. A quick jot on the back of an envelope and I can see that our students have produced at least 6000 pieces of work. And that's a conservative estimate! This anthology, therefore, is only a small sample of the huge body of work we have created. So, what has happened to the rest of the work? Some of the pieces found their way into one of our other anthologies: *There Is a Fire at the Heart of This City*, *A Confluence of Spaces*, *What If This Road*, and *This Is Your Life*. Other pieces have been performed on stage in Poetry Slams or recorded as lyrics within songs; some nestle inside beautiful hand-crafted journals; and some now exist only as stories inside our heads. I can still remember the hitchhiker climbing into the cab; a woman at work in a care home; a girl who lived above a butcher's shop. Brendan Pearson's novel and poetry collection has also been published before and extracts from these appear posthumously here. Brendan is much missed and we are very grateful to his family for allowing us to include his work in this anthology.

Even though I set prompts for each homework, each responding creation is unique with a strong authorial voice. I love the tangents, the swerves and the unexpected. From a lesson about folklore, the elegiac *Bears* by Esme Pears emerges alongside a haunting poem – *The Mystery of Coopers Hollow* - by Peter Watkins. In a homework on rap poetry, Diane Pilbro gets us into the groove with *How the Drum Helps*. Despite having a really difficult time recently, Mick Grant always managed to showcase his creative reading of the homework brief with funny stories of Clark Kent caught up in the modern world.

We enjoy our differences yet there are similarities too. Coincidences, you might say. Something in the air. For instance, although I never once set the theme of animals, they emerge. Caroline Izzard's *Come Out, Hedgehog!* and Esme's story above have animals in them. We also have Simon Black's filthy dog in *Mud* and Alan Vickers' oh-too-cute puppy in *Poppy*; Tess tells us how it is to be a cat; Kenny Mackay writes of owls and strange night-time creatures; Thomas Freestone cleverly uses a children's story about a bird to express how difference should be celebrated and Ankita Aggarwal writes of crows and flies. We also have mythical creatures and Hilli Thompson treats us to a story of a dragon. Nature too plays a huge part in Jan Addison's *Prospect,* Mai Black's *To a Raindrop*, and Sallyanne Webb's *Haven*. Each of these three poems gives us a unique vision of the world.

None of this work would be possible without a huge team of supporters cheering us on. Thank you so much to Inside Out Community team of which there are too many to mention in full but include Peter, Marie, Allan, Lois, Janice and all the crew at Inside Out Community. I get itchy eyes just thinking about all the hours Alan Vickers has put into typesetting and copy-editing it with Peter Watkins. Your sterling work is much appreciated. And finally, humungous thanks must go to all the contributors, not only for their pieces here, but for their hard work in class, their support of Write Minds, and their friendship. I hope you, the reader, get as much pleasure out of the work as I have.

Silver Birch.
In autumn light.
This heart at peace.

Brendan Wilson

Esther

This is the story of how Esther Jones, daughter of Larry and Alice Finklestein, brought peace to a small corner of the South Downs.

She felt as empty as this moonlit night: As barren as the fields: As bare as the stick branches. At this time of winter, Esther felt she might disappear altogether as she walked the familiar muddy path to the old stone that stood in the meadow just beyond the playing field. It was here at the ritual stone that the world on the edge of our consciousness came in to view. Where the action really happened. Esther mused that she might be the last of the Crones, Hags, Witches in these parts.

Every so often some teenagers would be there, drinking, smoking, picking mushrooms and a bad trip would ensue which would frighten them off until the next fools came through. But mostly the townsfolk had forgotten about this place, lost as they were in back-biting and commerce. She was safe for now.

It was bitter as she turned for home, fearing for the world. What would happen when she and those like her were all gone? Those of the old school who once populated and influenced this isle as much as the state-sponsored thought-police of today. Who would keep the balance then? As she turned the key a gentle drizzle fell; something will happen, she thought.

She ate the Prasada and drank the Great Spirit as she did every evening. All those tales of mischievous fairies causing trouble, she laughed, she'd never been caught in a ring or eaten the wrong food. Still she'd had some close shaves: earlier that day some boys had taunted and thrown mud at her, she'd shaken her stick at them and had sneered a fuck off. She saw them off all right but she sometimes feared she could be seriously hurt. Relax. She put Wagner on the phone her daughter had given her, "so we can stay in touch, so you won't be so lonely mum."

Esther woke in the armchair late morning. She rose awkwardly to answer a knock at the door. It was Dr Woodward, one of the local conscientious GPs with a woman she didn't recognise who introduced herself as Promise. "We've just popped around to see how you are," said Dr Woodward. "Can we come in…" and they marched into the living room past piles of newspapers and magazines, old cuddly toys, cereal packets, old photos and letters. Esther realised there was nowhere for them to sit down, but this was how she kept the score of the things around her. "We've just popped around," Dr Woodward said again, "just wanted to check that…"

"There was an incident yesterday afternoon. Some school boys, and a threat…" said Promise.

Three days later Esther was being helped, under the threat of a police escort, to a waiting car for a short drive to Fair Fields, God's waiting room on the hill. After three weeks of Countdown, gentle movement exercise and songs from the 1950s, she weakened. A week later her daughter, head bowed, followed the pallbearers into the chapel where the priest, God bless her, said a quick prayer and was satisfied.

As Esther slowly glided behind the blue velvet curtain, in a clear blue sky, rainbows appeared and a clear light entered the hearts of the men and women of the town and joy and satisfaction would last, as it turned out, for an incalculable length of time.

Love and Redemption

He'd always been there. As a toddler chatting away to her. At school always right behind her. Playing on the swings, he was dancing in front of her. She'd mentioned it to her best friend, Alice, but she had looked at her strangely and Jennifer never mentioned it again. At university, Ghoul as she simply called him, helped her find her way around the strange city when she was lost, told her what boys to avoid, which friendships to cultivate and even, she thought, answered some of the exam questions for her. It was Ghoul that suggested that she become a Librarian and that she write a novel. The novel had never got started but she enjoyed the library, especially the children and the old people, but especially the children. It was often Ghoul who persuaded her to spend money she didn't have on make up and perfume, on the occasional handbag. He nodded approvingly at a good hairstyle and looked disapprovingly if her skirt was too short.

Sometime around August of her 25th year she began to notice that Ghoul wasn't around and began to feel a bit lost. Her father was ill and they reduced her hours at the library to just three days and she was lucky to have that. Still no Ghoul. Jennifer couldn't afford the airy, high-ceilinged flat she loved, and her on and off relationship with Reece was over. She had tried, but she just couldn't love him and she didn't know why. He had buried himself in marijuana and computer games. It was for the best she told herself. Her school friend, Alice, was married with a baby and had no other ambition than to be adored. Her father died, just 62 and she moved to a basement room, which was where she was now staring at her distorted reflection in the mirror and crying.

She wept for her Father, for Reece, for her job, but mostly for Ghoul. In the end she cried so much that she forgot what she was crying about and it was only Thursday, four days until she was back at work. Nothing to do and no money to do it with, she sobbed even more. By the time Friday evening came around she was desperate.

Dressed up like a Tibetan against the cold, she walked the unfamiliar streets of Finsbury Park and continued to walk, until hungry and exhausted, she found herself outside a wine bar; counting her coins she stepped inside, into the busy warmth. At least she wouldn't be alone; eventually she found a stall by the window and cleared the condensation with a mitten and looked out onto the street at the rain and the reflections.

"Do you mind?" said a woman, gesturing to the seat next to Jennifer. She was old - she was young, smart with a bob of jet-black hair and an olive complexion.

"Not at all…Please…"

"You don't mind if I eat?" she continued with a perfect French accent and perfect English.

"No no…" whispered Jennifer.

"My mother says I eat like a pig… you hungry?" And she looked Jennifer up and down.

"You are hungry. Waiter!" she called and after a pause, "two rabbit stews and…" she turned towards Jennifer, "would you like more wine?" and Jennifer looked sheepish.

"A bottle of Medoc please thank you... it's so annoying that you can't smoke," and then addressing Jennifer she said, "What do you do?"

"I'm a Librarian," said Jennifer.

"Oh you are a writer?"

"Oh no just the odd poem here and there. You are a writer?"

"No, a reader."

And they talked of Virginia Woolf and Plath and Hannah Hoch, they were hard on Tracey Emin and loved the films of Steve McQueen.

"You are English?" questioned the woman.

"Yes," rather surprised. "My father was from Trinidad."

"Was?"

"Yes, he died not long ago."

"Oh I'm sorry."

"It wasn't your fault," replied Jennifer with a rye smile and they laughed a familial laugh.

"I'm French," said the woman ironically.

"No shit," said Jennifer and they laughed some more.

"My Grandmother was Algerian... she died too," and they silently drank the last of the wine.

Jennifer, needy and strong on the food and wine said "I don't live far away, would you like to come back for coffee?"

"I'll read you some poems," she offered with a happily expectant smile.

The rain had turned to sleet had turned to snow on the Blackstock Road and the tyres sprayed sludge over the pavement. The cold air sobered them as they hit the street.

"I'm Jennifer Blood, pleased to meet you. You can call me Jen."

"Henrietta. Henrietta Gall. At your service, mademoiselle." They walked arm in arm through the traffic and Jen found her way home somehow.

In the morning the basement was just that much lighter, that much warmer, a little less damp. Jen took a pen and an exercise book and sat at the small table. Henrietta slept like an angel as Jen wrote on the cover 'Love and Redemption a Ghost Story' and on the first page 'Chapter 1' and then 'It was love like no other that first night'. She paused. That was all so far. But Jen would write that novel, of that she was certain.

People of Ipswich

Day merges into night merges into day
Sun into rain into sun.
Come. Come.
Passed two women arm in arm.
Who pay attention to no one else.

And later I see them
As I stoop through the park.
Arguing.

Hugging.
Making up, holding hands

It's all the same where the penny lands.

TV politician, his profit and loss, the victor and vanquished.
The teacher with her right and wrong, good and bad.
The Priest, virtue and sin and heaven and hell.

None of us (let's admit it) really knows good that well.

So resist the would and the could and the should
And be kind and compassionate
In this small corner of the hood.

Jan Addison

Prospect

I drink you in
What pleasure you are giving me
Your sturdy yellow trumpets
Burst with sounds.
Break into the gloom of
Early morning.
Don't fade yet.
Keep on becoming
Hopefulness.

TREASURE
Family : noun; 1. People linked together by common ancestors 2. People who are bonded together by love

Caroline Izzard

How Can We Honour Our History Through Junk Journaling?

Blowing the dust off the old, battered cardboard shoebox handed to me by my mother, I was intrigued to find out what mysteries lay within. I lifted the lid to discover a disorganised jumble of beautiful, tatty, black and white, and sepia toned photographs of my family and ancestors. Also mixed up in the box were various papers commemorating births, deaths and marriages, and some scribbled notes with snippets of information like a jigsaw beckoning me to put the put the pieces together. I stepped up to the challenge asking myself, how can I transform this bundle of largely ignored and anonymous items into something coherent and beautiful that people would want to look at? What can I learn about the interconnecting lives that came before mine? How can I honour the value of the rich, meaningful existence of the people in the photographs, or the names on a page?

I decided to create a journal, or more specifically a 'junk journal' to incorporate the treasured history I was to uncover. A junk journal involves using what we have or would otherwise throw away to create a decorative book, folder or folio that can house anything of interest or meaning to the owner, and be written in in any way the heart desires.

My journal, in true Blue Peter spirit, was constructed of cereal box cardboard covered with collage pieces largely from a previous collection of papers given to me by my mother consisting of tickets, labels, postcards etc. that she had collected when she lived in France. These were further layered with my watercolour paintings of roses and butterflies and embellished with a range of items including fabric scraps, old buttons, broken jewellery and old book pages. I made copies of the photos and documents on my frankly inadequate printer as I did not want to use the originals just in case someone would prefer the dusty shoe box over my work of art! The items were cosily tucked into the various pockets and hidey holes provided for them in the journal.

Channelling my inner Sherlock Holmes, I sifted through the clues and started to build a more coherent picture of connections and relationships between the players in this drama of life. I found out that my great grandmother had gone into service at 13, and that my great-great- grandfather

inherited a fortune but gambled it all away. I tried to imagine what it would have been like to live through these experiences, and how their impact may have rippled out to those around them and trickled down through the ages.

So what human need am I fulfilling in undertaking this journey? From an evolutionary point of view we are biologically hardwired to form family bonds – forming attachments to those who can protect us and provide for us increases our chance of survival and therefore makes evolutionary sense. Those who share family lines will also share a proportion of our DNA, this makes them of interest to us as a way of passing those genes on through the generations. However, this does not neatly explain the interest in those who have come before us and have long since departed as they are no longer able to have any genetic value to us. It is maybe, therefore, more about the need for a sense of belonging and connection to something bigger than ourselves, enabling us to form an emotional link to family members who we have never met or even known of their existence. Family is also a big part of our identity and understanding where we came from may be a way of strengthening our understanding of who we are.

The process has enabled me to learn more about the roots and branches of my family and make sense of the muddle of information handed to me in that tatty cardboard box. It has opened up a conversation with my mother who happily reminisced details about her father fixing her toy pram and making her and her sister a mechanical Ferris wheel – treasured details that could so easily be lost with the passing of time. I have endeavoured to give context and meaning to the various photos and documents and clarify connections between them, thus awarding the lives lived the value they deserve. I hope I have created something special to be cherished and explored in years to come… and better than a battered old shoe box!

Come Out, Hedgehog!

“Hedgehog has rolled himself into a ball. How can we get him to come out?” asked Mouse.

“We could tell him to cheer up,” said Rabbit.
They told him to cheer up. Hedgehog did not come out.

“We could roll him around,” said Squirrel.
They rolled him around. Hedgehog did not come out.

“We could try to lift his head up,” said Badger.
They tried to lift his head up. Hedgehog curled up tighter.

“We could tickle him,” said Fox.
They tickled him. Hedgehog curled up tighter still.

“We could just sit with him and let him know we are here,” said Owl.
They just sat.

When Hedgehog was ready, he slowly uncurled until his little face peeped out from beneath the prickles.

“I just needed time,” said Hedgehog.
“We know,” said his friends.

"Hedgehog has rolled himself into a ball. How can we get him to come out?" Asked Mouse.

1.

"We could tell him to cheer up," Said Rabbit. They told him to cheer up. Hedgehog did not come out.

3.

2.

4.

"We could roll him around,"
Said Squirrel.
They rolled him around.
Hedgehog did not come
out.

5.

"We could try to lift his
head up," Said Badger.
They tried to lift his
head up.
Hedgehog curled up tighter.

7.

6.

8.

"We could tickle him,"
Said Fox.
They tickled him.
Hedgehog curled up tighter
still.

9.

10.

12.

When Hedgehog was ready
he slowly uncurled until
his little face peeped out
from beneath the prickles.

13.

14.

16.

Shifting Sands

Sunlight dances playfully
on the shimmering surface.
Calm, serene, beautiful.
Hiding the unconscious depths
that lurk beneath.
Immense, hidden, dark.
Ever-changing moods
that cannot be controlled.
The storm brings forth
a cathartic burst of energy and anger.
As it passes, peace fills the space
with no sorrow or remorse.
Tides breathe their ebb and flow.
Rise and fall.
Bringing forth new life
then taking it when turning to walk away.
The hooves of 100 white horses
thunder towards the shore,
spooked by the wind
entwining their manes.
Then come to rest
and replenish.
The view of the horizon
between sea and sky
brings hope.
A clear path to the future.
As mist descends to obscure the view
hope is lost.
The future fades.
This life is built on shifting sands.
Restless, ceaseless, endless cycles of change.
Over wrath and fury
we have no power
Just the wisdom watch and wait.

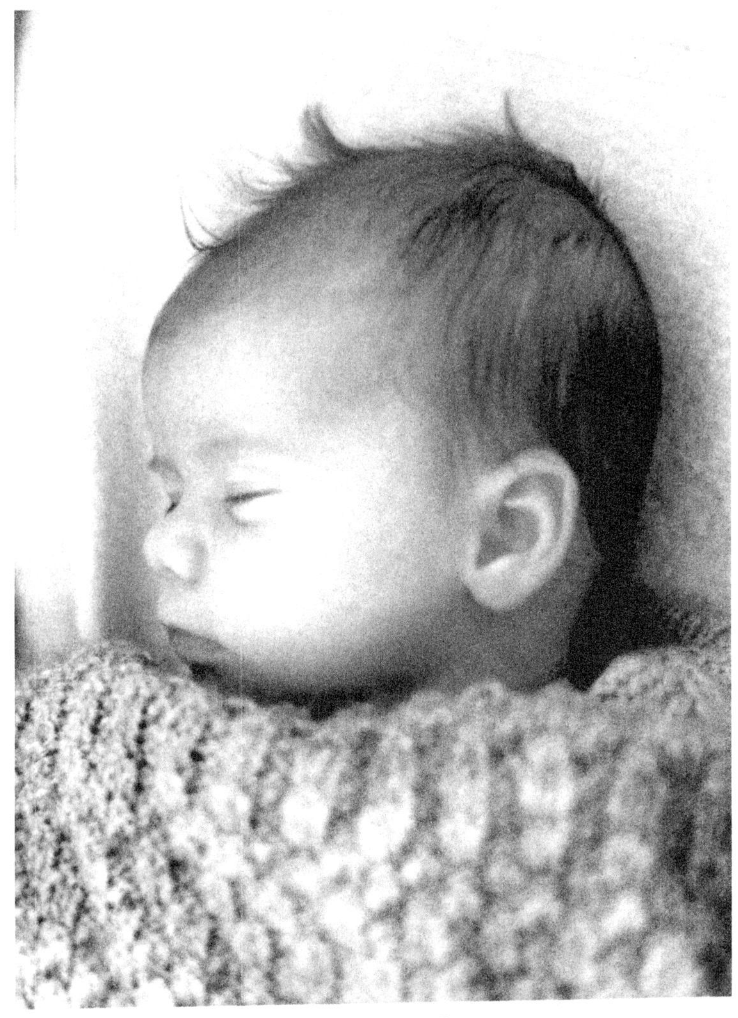

A sleeping baby
Seems to know the truth.
Peace.

Simon Black

Truth.

I see profound truth
When I look into the depth
Of a baby's eyes.

Mud

Mud
The dog tramples in it
Rolls around
Paws embedded
Tail bedraggled
Rain seeping down her back
Rivulets of sand and soil
She drinks water from the puddles
It hasn't done her any harm
(I might give it a go.)

The Abundant Chest

In a bus shelter, dark and cool
Was a wooden chest.
Just the right height
Strangely comfortable
I sat on it.
And there was a man
Dressed in silks
Chinese features
Walking towards me
An Emperor
Smiling, he said, "Look inside."
Then carried on walking, his silks brushing the ground gently.
I got up and looked inside
The box filled with jewels, gold, silver
As I scooped the jewels up, more appeared in the chest.
I filled my bag noticing that as I did the jewels were replaced
And the chest was overflowing
The jewels were priceless
I was a millionaire
Two weeks later
I thought of my Emperor
I drove my Rolls Royce to the bus shelter
Hoping to see and thank him
He appeared
His silks brushed the ground gently.
"I looked inside," I said. "Now I am richer than ever."
His face saddened

I even saw pity
"No, look inside," he said, tapping his chest
So I look inside myself
To the place where my heart is beating
And there in my chest is the peace that passes all understanding
And the smiling face of my Emperor.

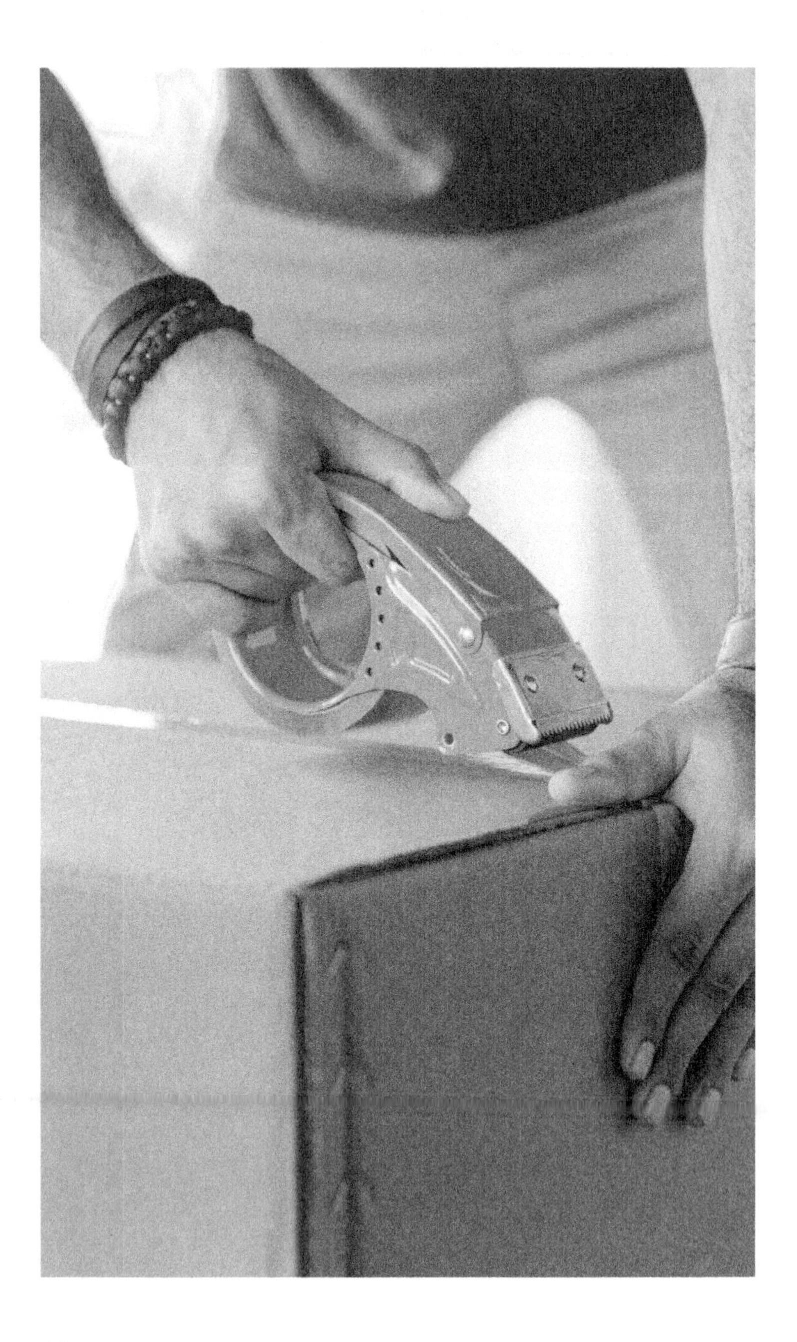

Alan Vickers

Hoarder

"But it's a broken iron!" she screamed. "I've already bought a new one. Why would *anyone* want to store a broken iron?"

He dipped one hand gingerly into the kitchen bin to retrieve it. "Well, you never know when..." he started.

"But it's *not* going to come in useful one day. You *know* that." She waved her hands in front of his face in a vain attempt to focus his attention. "And even in the unlikely event that it *might* come in handy one day in the far, far distant future, you won't be able to find then it anyway!"

He shrugged. "Look, it won't take up any space in a carrier bag in the under-stairs cupboard."

"No it won't," she said. "Because it's not bloody well going in there." She thought of the orderly rows of perfectly clean shoes that she'd arranged so neatly behind the under-stairs cupboard door - the door with the broken handle that he was supposed to have fixed two Christmases ago.

He tutted. "OK, fine. I'll just have to store it in my room."

"Oh no you don't. I haven't been able to hoover in there for weeks. I've forgotten what the carpet even looks like!" Her eyes flitted around the kitchen, from her beautiful cut-glass vase of fresh garden flowers on the window ledge, to the infuriating ever-dripping tap. She sighed as she looked him straight in the eye and said, calmly, "Listen, love. It's a broken iron. Please just get it shifted."

He recoiled from the uncomfortable eye contact and stomped across to the fridge, yanking open the squeaky door to stare at everything and nothing, and to feel the cold air on his face. He pressed his forehead into the hard edge of a shelf and, under his breath, he hissed "For God's sake." Then out loud, "Right. Fine. You win. I'll just have to buy another plastic box and store it in the garage."

She shouted at the back of his head. "With the other hundred or more plastic boxes you mean? Just listen to yourself. Can't you hear that you've got a problem?"

His jaw stiffened. "I have *not* got a problem." With his free hand, he grabbed a plastic milk carton and spun the lid free with his thumb - an action perfected after thousands of repetitions.

She sprang across the few feet of frayed carpet tiles and poked a hard finger repeatedly into his bicep to punctuate her point. "Well I've asked you nicely every single day for over ten years to start throwing this useless old tat away, and you completely refuse to see sense."

He ignored the physical assault and made a defiant show of swigging greedily from the milk bottle before returning it to the door and wiping his mouth on his sleeve.

"Nagged," he said.

"What?" She drew her neck back and cocked her head.

"Nagged," he repeated, turning slowly to meet her gaze. "You haven't asked nicely; you've nagged. You've nagged me every single day for over ten years. Do you know what that feels like?"

She looked up at the crumbling plaster and flaky paint of the ceiling, clenched her fists at the end of stiff arms and vented a silent scream of exasperation.

"Oh don't be so dramatic," he rolled his eyes, then continued to stare at her with well-honed impassivity until she felt compelled to look back at him again. He adopted a patronising tone. "Anyway, you'll be pleased to know that I've found a solution to your little problem. If you think you could just calm down for ten seconds, then I might be able to tell you."

She glared at him and waited.

He let the silence grow for a few long seconds as he slowly closed the fridge door, then said "OK, the other day, I rang a professional offsite storage company and got a quote for them to store all the boxes. So you won't need to constantly nag, nag, nag me any more. You can totally reclaim my man-drawer. You can do what you like with the under-stairs cupboard. You can hoover my room if you must. And you can even get your precious car into the garage as that seems to be so important to you. I tell you what - I'll go on a diet too so that even *I* take up less room in my own house! Happy now?"

She stared at him and crossed her arms. Then she asked, firmly, "How much?"

"Never you mind about that." He barged past her and leaned on the chipped draining board, talking to the garden rather than directly to her. "Believe me, it's money well spent to stop your nagging. Oh, and don't get me wrong... I'm sure you'll work hard to find some other reason to nag me, but at least you won't be able to nag me about storage ever again."

"How much?" she asked again.

He turned away from the window. "Well, it's quite good value considering the number of boxes, and it's also completely secure and confidential, so no-one will ever be able to stick their noses in and interfere with my stuff."

"How much?" she insisted, raising her voice in ultimatum.

"Just over £100 a month" he said, casually rubbing his nose, "and they can start this Saturday."

Her face flushed red. "Stop right there! Enough is enough!" she spitted through gritted teeth. "If you *dare* start spending £100 a month of *our* money storing your stupid junk for absolutely no good reason, then we're finished. Do you understand that?"

She glanced from the gleaming hob and spotless work surfaces to the disassembled radio that she always knew, despite his earnest promises, would never be fixed. "And do you know what else? I'll damn well take you to the cleaners in the divorce courts for unreasonable behaviour. You'll finally be out of this house and out of my life. You'll be lucky if you're left with £100 a month to spend on food and rent." She laughed hysterically, her eyes wild and wet. "What will you do with your precious clutter then, eh?" With one swipe of her forearm, she scattered the broken radio parts onto the floor. "Well I hope you'll be very happy together. You *bloody* fool. You utter... *loser*!" She turned her back, leaned her head against the door jamb and started to sob.

He felt the weight of the broken iron in his hands and looked across at the bin. Options flashed through his thoughts in a whirl of confusion, followed by cold calm clarity. Without even consciously thinking it through, he knew what he must do to restore the peace in this marriage.

***

The next morning, he rang the storage company. "Hello, yes, this is Mr Collins. I called a couple of days ago about the short term storage of around 120 large plastic boxes, and you quoted me £149. Yes, well, I'm sorry to mess you about but there's been a change of circumstances. I discussed it with my wife, and I'm afraid we need to cancel that order..." He waited until the remote sound of keyboard clacking stopped.

"While I'm on though, could I get you to quote me for another requirement? OK, great, thanks. Yes, could you please quote me for the long-term storage of a single secure box... Yes... just one. The size? Hang on..."

He looked down at the crumpled mess on the kitchen floor, next to the broken, and now stained iron that he knew would come in handy one day.

"Well... I reckon about 6ft by 2ft by 2ft ought to cover it."

Poppy

And so he woke, head banging from another long and drunken evening spent alone. The short, fitful, fretful, night was over. Endured, if not enjoyed. He rubbed the sleep from his eyes as he adjusted to the gloomy light diffusing through the curtains - the curtains that she had chosen.

Every day had been pretty much the same since the funeral. Months had passed and Pete Turner had not adjusted well to life without Kate. Apart from the obvious big-picture vacuum of love and companionship, he also felt her absence in myriad tiny ways throughout every hour of every day. He felt that he had little to live for and so he'd slowly slipped and settled into a joyless existence of aching drudgery and misery.

He lamented that he'd not kept in touch with the friends that he'd made as a single man in his 20s. In later married life, most of their friends were her friends really, so now they had no reason to contact him.

He scratched his scalp and decided again not to bother with a shower. He sighed and pulled on his trousers that had lain overnight on the floor next to their bed. There wouldn't be much point in a shower anyway - he'd used the last of the shower gel a few days back and hadn't thought to replace it. Kate had always been the one to buy stuff like that. Besides which, what did it matter if he smelled a little bit musky - he wasn't planning to be close to anyone and he was becoming quite familiar, and even fond of his own natural odour.

A few weeks ago, in a rare moment of lucidity and self-awareness, he'd booked an appointment to see the doctor and felt both embarrassed and strangely relieved to have cried for the first time in front of a stranger. The doctor had urged him to stop self-medicating with alcohol and to try a course of anti-depressants. After a couple of weeks on the pills, Pete did feel some vestige of an improvement to his mental well-being, but he decided it wasn't enough to stop the drinking too.

***

Mr Patel's Mini-Mart opened at 10am and Pete was waiting outside as usual. One of the many Patel children pushed a hand through the blinds to flip the sign from Closed to Welcome and unbolted the glass door.

Two minutes later, a flimsy carrier bag strained with the weight of four cans of Polish super-strength lager, two Indian veggie samosas, Italian salami on a French baguette, and a Cornish pastie. He had quite the cosmopolitan elevensies to look forward to as he headed towards the park. He cracked open the first can and drank as he walked. There was a bin about 600 yards down the road, which he'd learned was perfectly placed for the disposal of his first empty of the day.

He relished the first rush of numbness as the alcohol seeped into his system. He surrendered to the familiar, fuzzy, comforting detachment from reality. His first level shield was successfully deployed and he was ready to endure the day.

At the park, Pete sat down onto his usual bench and placed the carrier bag beside him. The bench was long enough for perhaps three or four people, but no-one had yet shared it with him. He knew he gave off the wrong signals for that. He hoped so anyway.

He'd learned that the best thing about this particular bench was the thickness of its wooden legs. They were slightly wider than the circumference of a can so it was easy to be discreet. He took a long swig from the second can and then rested it on the floor as he leaned back to take in the familiar scene.

In the far distance, the trees behind the river swayed in harmony as they danced to the gentle breeze. The river itself was several shades of grey ribbon that intertwined and oscillated as the high tide turned. A few boats bobbed on their moorings as couples walked along the muddy path on the nearside raised bank - couples like Pete and Kate had been. He heard the distant shouting and laughter of happy children playing in the council playground and sighed at their innocence. He envied their blissful ignorance of the hardships to come in later life. Poor kids.

In the grassy foreground he watched a groundsman lean

forwards as he struggled to push a rusty old wheeled contraption that marked out the white lines of a junior football pitch.

He saw a woman talking into her mobile phone whilst walking a small dog that strained ahead against its lead. As he watched, the woman stumbled on the uneven ground, and her phone was dislodged from her hand. She made a frantic grab to try to catch the flying phone and inadvertently let go of the dog lead. The liberated animal sprinted away from her and scampered in a large arc that quickly resolved into a straight line heading directly towards Pete.

***

The tiny fluffy dog, no more than ten inches high, slowed and approached at a canter, its lead trailing behind in the damp grass, then it stopped abruptly about two yards away. It panted, lopped out its tongue, cocked its head, and stared up at Pete. Its tail wagged furiously and its round head bobbed down intermittently. Pete realised that it was looking for some confirmation or permission that it was OK to come closer.

Without really thinking, Pete dropped his right hand down below the bench seat and dangled his fingers. That was apparently the signal the dog was waiting for as it rushed forward and nudged its cold moist nose against Pete's fingers. It flicked its head to raise Pete's hand a little, and then nuzzled its whole head underneath Pete's palm and pressed into his warm grip. Then it stretched its neck so that Pete's hand slipped down to the dog's shoulders, and Pete realised that it was training him how to stroke it.

He took the hint and slid his hand firmly but gently down the dog's back, through the off-white tufty fur, then lifted it to return to the head and repeat the motion. The little dog seemed to relish the experience, and Pete was surprised that he too was touched by the intimacy. He felt a smile appear unbidden on his normally stoic face. The muscles ached through under-use.

After about a minute, the woman approached them slowly, probably trying to work out whether or not her dog was annoying the stranger, but also happy to see it petted and appreciated.

"He's a lovely little thing," said Pete, looking up as he continued to stroke the contented dog.

"Oh, he's a she, actually," said the woman, smiling. "She's called Poppy."

Pete glanced down and saw that all the clues were there - the lurid pink lead; the diamanté collar; and, as the dog rolled onto her back for a tummy tickle, Pete saw the indisputable biological proof. He flushed a little and said "Ah... yes... of course she is..." and smiled back up at the woman.

The woman held out her hand and announced her name. It was something like Linda or Sandra. Pete remembered that it had two syllables anyway. His attention was still fully focused on Poppy as he muttered "I'm Peter. Pete. Nice to meet you."

Pete suddenly felt self-conscious about the can standing by his feet and wondered if his breath might reek of alcohol. He nonchalantly moved the can a few inches behind the leg of the bench and continued to stroke the tiny appreciative creature at his feet.

"Come on then Poppy," said Linda/Sandra as she bowed down and clapped her hands together at knee level. "Come on! Dinner time!"

Poppy looked back and cocked her head inquisitively. Then the dark wet pools of her eyes looked back up at Pete for a fraction of a second before she head-butted his calf and bounded off to run ahead of the woman, excited by the prospect of food.

To his surprise, Pete laughed out loud and held his hand up to wave goodbye to Poppy. Linda/Sandra waved back at him with a broad smile on her face.

***

When Pete got home, he noticed again the unpleasant smell that he'd somehow managed to ignore, and he decided that it was time he sorted out the washing-up. So he gathered all the crusty plates, bowls, mugs, and cutlery from the work surfaces, from the sink, from the living room, and from the downstairs toilet, and he loaded them all into the dishwasher. He was pleasantly surprised at how quickly it was done. He'd been dreading the difficulty of the task for weeks, and so hadn't felt motivated to even start.

***

Next morning, Pete woke to find that he was already thinking about dear little Poppy. He lay there with a smile beaming across his face as he remembered the previous day's encounter.

He wondered if he might come across Poppy again today. People like routine don't they? Perhaps Linda/Sandra takes Poppy for a walk at the same time every day? Well it would be easy to put this theory to the test.

Pete rolled out of bed and picked up his trousers from the bedroom floor. As he pulled them up past his knees, he stopped and reconsidered. He glanced around the room, not focusing on anything in particular as he weighed up the possibilities for the day ahead. His mind made up, he kicked off the trousers, quickly followed by his underpants and T-shirt, then fended off the goose-bumps by gathering his arms and fists close to his chest and tip-toed naked into the cold bathroom to turn on the shower. Plain water was probably better than nothing, he thought. Later on he'd buy some shower gel or shampoo or whatever.

As he left the house, he glanced at the front lawn and really saw it for the first time in ages. He might tackle the grass cutting this afternoon. It had grown to about 18 inches high, so he'd probably have to scythe or shear it down before he could attack it with the mower. Shouldn't be a problem though.

He patted down the front of the blue shirt that he'd ironed, nodded to himself, and set off for the park at a reasonable pace. He took a more direct route rather than the diversion past Mr Patel's. For one thing, he was keen to install himself on the bench well before Poppy arrived, and for another, he didn't much fancy his morning cans today. Maybe later.

His luck was in. After an interminable half-hour of restless fidgeting on the bench, and a constant struggle to resist the nagging urge to run back to Mr Patel's, he was relieved to see Poppy and the woman appear in the far corner of the big field. As they made their way across the grass, Pete sat upright and tried to catch their attention without being too obvious. As Sandra/Linda glanced in his direction, he raised his right hand to signal "hello again," She might have smiled, but Pete didn't really notice as his attention was drawn to the darling little Poppy as she too glanced in his direction and then started to tug at her lead to drag her human over to see this interesting new human again.

"Well she certainly likes you!" said Sandra/Linda as she trotted behind, only able to stop once Poppy had reached Pete and had settled in for an invigorating scritch-scratch.

Sandra/Linda dropped the lead and sighed contentedly as she lowered herself to sit on the bench next to Pete.

They engaged in polite small-talk for a few minutes, mostly instigated by Linda/Sandra as Pete and Poppy kept each other entertained in constant indulgent contact.

***

So was forged the pattern of the next few days. Linda/Sandra would stop to rest on Pete's bench for five or ten minutes while Pete petted Poppy and skilfully ignored her attempts to start proper conversations. Pete had become an expert in appearing friendly, polite, and engaged without ever revealing anything dangerously real about himself. But Pete thought that Linda/Sandra shouldn't feel troubled by not knowing much about him; after all, he didn't even know her proper name.

***

For several evenings in a row, Pete had mulled over ways in which he could engineer some more time with Poppy. He supposed the most obvious way; the way that normal people would choose; would be to simply ask Sandra/Linda if he could perhaps take Poppy for a walk sometime. But he cringed at the thought. Would it seem a bit weird? What if she were offended? Or embarrassed? What if it made things awkward? Maybe he'd get to see even less of Poppy…

In the event, his anxiety was unnecessary, as there came a day when she actually asked him. He was sitting on the bench as normal, when Sandra/Linda rushed up to him in a bit of a fluster, virtually dragging poor Poppy along by a short taut lead.

"Hi there," she panted "Look, I'm sorry to ask, but I wonder... would mind doing me a little favour?"

"Sure!" He sat up straight and looked up at her blotchy reddened face while simultaneously dropping his right arm down to cup under poppy's throat for a quick and evidently welcome rub. "How can I help?"

"Oh, great, thanks! Well, I just need to pop into the surgery for a few minutes and I forgot that they don't allow dogs in there. Stupid idiot! I could tie her up outside but she hates that and she'll make a fuss with all the crying and barking and so..."

"Look. Stop. It's fine. No need to explain. You just get off and do what you need to do. We'll be fine here won't we Poppy, eh? Yes, we will won't we, eh? Yes we will."

Pete enveloped Poppy's face with both warm palms and rotated his wrists so that he felt the beautiful tufty fur rub past his fingers. Poppy's eyes widened as his hands stretched her skin in every direction, and she licked her lips in utter pleasure.

He looked up again at Sandra/Linda, smiled, and cocked his head as a signal that it was fine for her to go.

She lingered for a fraction of a second as if finally

weighing up the right decision, then she flashed a quick smile at both Pete and Poppy before trotting off in the direction of the Doctors. She shouted over her shoulder, "I'll literally be about ten or fifteen minutes. Twenty minutes tops!"

"No worries!" shouted Pete. "You just take as long as you need." Then in a whisper down at Poppy, "Or preferably much, much longer, eh?"

As soon as Sandra/Linda was out of sight, Pete tapped twice on his thighs and, to his delight, Poppy leaped into his lap in a single athletic bound. She sat back on her hind legs and planted both front legs on Pete's shoulders as she proceeded to energetically lick his face. He recoiled his face in mock horror as if trying to avoid the attack but, secretly, he was loving it. The more he laughed, the more Poppy licked. Her tongue was simultaneously abrasive and moist, and it was the most sensual, intimate interaction he'd experienced with another living thing in ages. He felt alive. Vital.

Pete decided to distract Poppy with a tickle, and it worked in an instant. After just two rubs of her pink, downy underbelly she ceased the licking and rolled over onto her back to grant Pete unfettered access to the glorious tickle zones.

"Oh, I do love you, Poppy," said Pete in a low calming voice as he transitioned the tickling and scritch-scratching into a slow, relaxing stroke.

At this, Poppy stood unsteadily on his thighs, like a newborn Bambi, and rotated her body round a couple of times before settling down into a sleeping position, with her nose snuggled into his crotch.

Pete looked down at the warm bundle of love, felt the tiny heart beating against his thigh, and experienced a surge of well-being spreading through his veins and fuelling the broad smile that spread across his contented face - a proper smile - one that shone through his eyes as well as his mouth.

After several minutes of mutual contentment, Pete was shocked back into the real world as Poppy jerked up her head and raised her ears. It was several seconds later that Pete too heard the familiar cadence of Sandra/Linda's walk as she approached from behind.

"Sorry!" she shouted, " It took a bit longer than I was expecting... Sorry, sorry, sorry."

"Look, it's no problem," said Pete. "We've had a great time sitting here, haven't we, Poppy?"

He spread his thighs a little wider so that Poppy tumbled through the gap and onto the grass below. She sneezed a couple of times and recovered her posture via a rapid shake of her fur that spiralled and spread seamlessly from head to body to tail.

Sandra/Linda leaned down to pick up Poppy's lead that lay limp on the grass.

"Oh, thanks again. You're such a sweetie," she said. "You're a life-saver In fact!... Will we see you again tomorrow then?" She waited patiently until Pete realised that he'd been asked a question and said "Oh, erm, yes. See you tomorrow then. Bye Poppy!" He ruffled the fur on Poppy's head as they both turned and made off in the direction of town.

***

The next morning, Pete was horrified to see that he was running late. He'd spent longer than planned packing up some of Kate's clothes and non-sentimental belongings into bags to take to a charity shop at the weekend.

Anxious that he might miss his daily rendezvous with Poppy, he decided to take the most direct route via the main road in an effort to head them off at the pass, as it were.

As he half-walked, half-trotted, down the final couple of hundred yards, Pete heard a familiar voice shouting from behind on the opposite pavement. It was Linda/Sandra, and she was yelling "Poppy! No!" Pete saw that she'd dropped a carrier bag onto the pavement. In that same moment, Poppy had pulled the lead from her hand and was now racing across the road to greet him.

***

The next couple of seconds played out in ultra-slow-motion and Pete became hyper-aware of every sensory detail.

He saw Poppy bounding across the verdant grass verge, her garish pink lead flapping and trailing free beneath her tiny body. Her tail wagged furiously as she leaped down from the kerb, over the grimy gutter, and onto the dirty black tarmac road.

Her head nodded and her ears perked up in excitement as she met his gaze and emitted two short, friendly barks of salutation.

He was vaguely aware of the muffled sound of distant traffic as Poppy crossed the centre line of the road, now just six or seven yards away from a stroke, and a scritch-scratch, and a face-lick, and a snuggle.

Then he heard the sharp piercing sound of squealing brakes to his right, loud and close. In his peripheral vision he saw the shape of a full-size coach bearing down on Poppy as she encroached the near-side carriageway.

Pete thought he saw the slightest turn of her head as the dark shadow of the coach enveloped Poppy but, mercifully, before she could even register what was happening, it had already happened.

Pete instinctively closed his eyes tight, and grimaced as he turned his head away.

But he could do nothing to block out the sounds.

The sharp dry sound of cracking bones.

The blunt wet sound of squashing flesh and organs.

The popping, splashing sound of skull and brain as they transitioned in an instant from three dimensions to two.

The abrasive sound of hot stinking rubber sliding across tarmac.

The chilling sound of the unearthly scream emitted from Sandra/Linda as she fell to her knees on the opposite pavement.

The echoing memory of the sound of Poppy, barking in loving innocent excitement less than a second before.

The internal sounds of his own violent retching and sobbing.

These were the sounds that would haunt Pete Turner in the few hours that remained of his own distraught life.

The Hall of Mirrors

You walk slowly through the hall of mirrors
staring at yourself in each

This mirror makes you look fat
The disgusting gross bulge in your midriff
dominates the first impression

This mirror twists your chest
Your heart is distorted and warped
All emotion pinched and squeezed
to death

This mirror enlarges your head
Deforms your face
Greasy embryonic black-heads take centre stage
Poor pores
Sick skin
Your mouth contorted downwards
in a sad, disagreeable sneer

This mirror creates a mess of your hair
An unwashed tangle of unkempt tufts
A stranger to brushes
and dye

This mirror drains all colour from your skin
You stand there, grey as grey
All vitality faded
All life desaturated

This mirror blurs you out completely
The background shines through
You all but disappear
Nothing worthy of notice

This mirror makes you appear to stoop
Pitiful posture
Bent and downtrodden
As if to bear the weight of the world

This mirror exaggerates your staring eyes
Red veins criss-cross the bulging yellow sclera
Dark pupils expose the haunted soul within
Gateways to a troubled mind

You stare some more

You look down

At the bottom of each mirror
A message jolts you back

NOW WASH YOUR HANDS

You leave the public toilet

They were mirrors

Just normal mirrors

Tess Last

A Kitten's Life

Just woke up from a gentle snooze dreaming of mice. Urgh, what is this? I've come outside for a play and business, and everywhere is covered in white stuff. It's very cold and it's falling through the air, covering my nose and whiskers. I shake it off but more replaces it. I go down the garden, the stuff sticking to my toes. It looks very pretty, so I have a roll, getting nice and wet.

In through the cat flap and straight onto my human's lap. They don't seem too impressed with me putting the white stuff all over their dry jumper, but I don't care; it's my human and my house. The human puts me on the floor and rubs me with a cloth, which I quite enjoy. All the time they are muttering and moaning about the white stuff.

Later on, after another nap, I'm pleased to see a litter tray, as I really don't fancy the white stuff again. I curl up on my human's lap and listen while they discuss the white stuff, which apparently is called snow!

Kenny Mackay

Three Little Owls.

It was my friend Dan who told me about the three little owls that perch on the limb of the old Oak tree just by the paddocks where you can pick up horse manure. But I had never seen them until yesterday. While walking along the Lane near sunset, I came across a young boy staring up at the tree and asking questions.

"Who set the horse manure afire?" he was asking to the tree. "I have to know."

This unusual scene drew my attention. And the horse manure looked like it was burning not just steaming. I could not see who he was talking to but as I got closer, I could see the owls. Three of them. Perched side by side where the long branch stretches out into the paddock.

"Come on, tell me. You must know. Owls are wise and know everything."

The young boy was getting more and more exasperated as the owls refused to answer.

"Maybe these three little owls are not as wise as their cousins the barn owls," I said.

"But it is not a big question," the little boy said. "So even a silly little owl should know the answer. And owls are wise.

They see everything."

Now everyone knows that owls are wise and so the little boy's enquiry made perfect sense. I often wondered myself 'How did the horse manure burn and smoke some days but not others?' Indeed, I also wondered who set it ablaze? Was it the owner? Was it some passing hooligan? It was a bit of a puzzle. But I never thought to ask the owls - that did not make much sense to me, as an adult. I knew all about anthropomorphication.

But why were owls considered to be wise? Is it because their heads can turn 360 degrees so that they can see in all directions? Is it because they fly completely silently so nobody knows they are there, and so the owls can hear everybody's secrets? Owls can see in the daytime and also when hunting at night, so nothing is hidden from them; they know everything.

All of a sudden, the little boy grew quiet as if he was listening. And then he turned away and began to walk down the lane towards the cottages. After a few steps, he broke out into a run, and his blue jumper and red shorts disappeared completely from sight. So, I didn't get to ask him if he had got his reply from the owls. Silly thing to think I know… And I was much too sensible and grown up to ask the owls myself.

So, it is still a mystery who sets fire to the horse manure stack down Seven Cottages Lane.

Late Night Messenger

The late-night flickering on my screen
is interrupted by a harsh barking
that is neither dog nor cat nor human.
Insistent, raucous, guttural.
The midnight moon illuminates only partially
and safety lights are triggered
by my presence outside the front door.
They don't help, with their intense blinding light -
revealing only what I already know
to be there in the garden.
I move outside the arc of this unseeing
and gaze longingly into the mirky darkness
that hangs along the road.
And the gruff barking comes again.
So my presence hasn't scared it off.
But where, and what is it?
It's not far off, it's close by.
But its form is not entrusted to me
and I know I will only hear it tonight:
a fuller apprehension will not be mine.
One last look from the front door
offers a household cat trotting
along the crown of the quiet night road.
Tail to snout - a horizontal line of purpose.
Emerging from the source of the sound,
he has encountered the barking being.
But intent on hunting, he hurries on
and tells me nothing of his encounter.
So back indoors, having heard the messenger,
the message is still a mystery.

Persephone Returns.

Acheron. Cocytus Square. Phlegethon Boulevard. Lethe. Styx corner. The stations were coming thick and fast now. She was not looking forward to returning to her possessive mother. The heat in the subway carriage was stifling. The sunlight dazzling every time they came out of a tunnel. Her Ray-Bans could protect her eyes but nothing could ward off the intense heat on her skin. She'd never got used to this transition. It troubled her beauty. Her cheeks flushed like pomegranates.

She turned to the teenage girl sitting to her right. All dressed in black. A strange darkness exuding from her, that matched the colour of long tresses that fell down one side of her face. The other side was shaven, revealing the pride of her tattoos. Black leather jacket. Black leather boots. Both studded with metal spikes.

"Melanie, are you are you sure you packed everything?"

"Yes, Mom," answered the girl.

It didn't look like it - one Fjall Raven hand sack and a 4-wheeled cabin bag that would fit into the smallest Ryanair overhead locker.

"Have you still got a signal?"

"Yes, Mom."

"Tell your dad we're nearly there."

The daughter's fingers danced on the small iPhone screen. 'Ping' sounded.

"Done."

At least the three hounds were not sulking, even if they could. They would miss the Eleusinian Fields but other pastures would suffice for them. Demeter's harsh tongue was rarely directed to them. She saw them as the hounds of Hades, and would do her best to pretend that they had not come back with her daughter. Demeter hated everything that reminded her of her daughter's spouse, anything that reminded her of the half year Persephone spent in her husband's world. And away from her. He'd never been the right sort for her daughter. He didn't look or act like one of the three most powerful men on the planet. And Demeter had insisted that she couldn't or wouldn't maintain proper order of the family's mysterious activities without her daughter beside her. And so the yearly ritual ascent uptown in spring to be with her mother, followed by the descent in fall, to be with her husband was negotiated. The hounds were surety of this.

"You know you will get on fine with her."

"Yes, Mum."

"Well what's the matter?"

"Owww. You know she doesn't really like me. It's always the same....and I can't even mention Dad's name without a tantrum."

"Aaaww, come here darling..."

"Muuum. I'm not a child."

The second teenager, a sinuous lad, toyed with the three hounds. Quietly. Attentive to their rumbles and silent demeanour, never straying from play to torment. As lean and languorous as the hounds themselves, a wild thing, his limbs relaxed but poised for motion.

City Hall Station arrived as always. No-one on the platform. It was only ever open twice a year. Only ever open for her. For Persephone's return and Persephone's departure.

'Derrid, derrid, derrid derrid. Derrid derrid, derrid. Shoooosh.'

To the other inhabitants of the subway train the family of three looked slightly otherworldly. Didn't look as if they had to ride the subway every day under the compulsion of the Yankee dollar. And their clothes... From a different time... Clearly designer, hand made. Majestic. And they seemed to transform into lighter hues as each of the trinity stepped out of the carriage onto the platform.

'Derrid, derrid. Derrid, derrid. Derrid, derrid.'

"Funny. Totally weird. Never seen that station before," said one passenger to her companion as the train pulled away from the old City Hall Station.

Mick Grant

What Is He Like?

Clark Kent put his mobile down. "Loïs, Murphy says he knows nothing about it, but he knows someone that was there when it happened."

"Oh yes? What's his name?"

"He wouldn't say."

"You didn't ask him," Loïs said, sharply.

That was true enough; however, Clark knew that asking would have done no good; a lot like asking Loïs to be patient with him one week in four. He made a note-to-self to ask her why, but not this week. "You want me to push him for-"

"No!" she snapped. "I know Murphy can be a waste of skin sometimes. We need to tread carefully, more than usual for him."

"Have there been any more attacks?"

"Not that I know about in the last few days. I don't like it at all."

"Murphy did say to meet him outside Central Station in an hour."

"That's promising. He doesn't do anything without a good reason," Loïs said.

"Sometimes a waste of skin, sometimes a case solver. We

need to get going."

"You're right. It's not like we can fly there."

Clark and Loïs stepped out onto the street a few minutes later. He heard heavy breathing and felt something gooey hit his face from forehead to chin. He saw a woman running away. He thought quickly. This was clearly the Custard Pie attacker; he could get her easily but not without giving himself away. Loïs was cleaning her own face. He didn't laugh. Much. "Did you get a look at her face, Loïs? She's wearing a green I heart NY t-shirt and has run up the next street on the left."

"How can you tell that? Your glasses are covered in goop, and you're still wearing them."

Shit. He took his glasses off to clean them of the gooey mess left by the custard pie attack on his face. Loïs laughed. Clark sucked the slop into his mouth. "Tastes good."

"How did you know which way the woman went? For that matter, how do you know it was a woman?"

Clark swallowed the pie topping and put as little as he could into licking the lenses. He did not want to break the glasses with his supertongue, and he hoped that Loïs would forget her line of questioning. He could hope.

"Come on, superhero, out with it."

She had worked it out. "Out with what, Loïs? Superwhat did you call me?" Bluff it out, like the editor did.

"Superhero. It would take someone with superpowers to look through those glasses. You're blushing."

Clark had heard of blushing but had not known what it was. Now he did. It was something to do with cleaning glasses with the tongue. "Of course I'm blushing. I've got to clean my glasses somehow."

"What are you talking about? Sorry about the superhero bit. A superhero wouldn't think blushing would clean glass."

"I wouldn't? I mean, he wouldn't?"

"Or she," Loïs said in a lower tone.

Clark's shoulders dropped slightly. "Or she." He was about to ask what blushing was, but that might make him seem stupid. Then again, that would take Loïs way off the scent.

"So how do you know where the attacker went?"
"Wait," Clark said. "This lens needs extra blushing."
""'ve got it!" Loïs said, a few decibels louder.
"Got what?"
"My brother had some sixth sense. It came with his Aspergers, and he could hear ultrasound. You're autistic, aren't you?" There was a softness to her voice.
Clark had no idea what Loïs was talking about, but that was only good right now. He could read up on it. "That's right; I've got some asparagus." He looked at her in time to see her shake her head slowly.

***

Sheena left the bus at the nearest stop to her home, or would have done if she had remembered to get off outside the flats. The next nearest had to do. No matter. She was still excited from the thrill of the day. She made her way into the flat called Casa Sheena, wishing as always that she had been named Blanca. Maybe one day she will have it changed.
"Is that you, Dinner?" a woman said from the sitting room.
Oh yes. The endless reminder that she said, once too often, "Call me what you like, as long as it's not 'Late for dinner'."
"You're back early, aren't you, Supper?" Two can play at that game.
"No. I said I'd be home on the ninth."
"Oh yeah." Sheena walked into the sitting room. "I've been thinking today was Tuesday. How was it?"
"The usual with Dad, but Sarah's dementia is worsening. Do you know where my squirty cream got to?"
"Um. Yes. I made a cake for that dishy guy in the office block I told you about."
"You did what?" Supper stood up and rushed to hug her lodger. "Well done you. I thought you would never do anything about him."
"I know. Little Miss Shy. I thought about what you said

your sister did, and got on with it. I wanted the thrill she got. I'll replace the cream, of course."

"Have it on me. Well, how did he take it? Are there other plans?"

"Thank you. I like to think so. Now that I've done that, I can do more. I wish I'd done it sooner."

"You did it at all. That's the main thing. What happened after you gave him the cake?"

Sheila flopped into the bean bag, smiling. "Well-"

"Wait a minute," Supper said, warily. "You said you did what Beth did. You cheeky little…"

"Tina will you stop all that clacking with your keyboard?" Gary shouted.

"Wow, don't you sound angry?" Tina shouted back.

"You"d be angry, too, if you had that tap tap tap CLACK tap tap tap CLACK going on in your face!"

"It is going in my face and yours is the other side of the office, and anyway, it never bothered you before."

The other workers had stopped their chatter. One of them took her phone into the stationery cupboard to talk in there.

"It's bothering me now!" Gary roared.

"Why don't both go outside for a smoke and cool down?" said Perry, not much quieter than them.

"Yes, Editor, sir!" the two warriors shouted, as they raced for the door. They high-fived as they met.

"How stupid do they think I am? Shirley, please print those two letters of dismissal for me."

"With pleasure, Perry," Shirley said with a forced laugh.

"Listen up, everyone," Perry said. "The government has ordered a lockdown of social interaction."

"They've done what?"

Perry knew from months with Sara to ignore her protests of faked ignorance. "We're having to change the way we work. From now until June, we will be working from home."

"Coronavirus."

"Yes, Loïs. We don't want to be like Italy."

"You mean swimming in olive oil?" Sara smirked. "And

all thanks to some old bat in China."

"Pack up your gear, all of you, and sign out your laptops. And Sara, you take a warning for racism."

The stationery cupboard door opened. Someone stepped out, holding a phone. "Where's everyone gone?"

***

Clark whistled the tune he had heard a busker singing outside the office. He poured the water from the kettle and into the mugs on the tray, before taking it to the three women in the sitting room. He brushed his left arm against the door frame with his right arm at the 35.7° angle, tapped his left foot three times against the tall light that was five and two-thirds inches from the skirting board. He walked forward north by east northwest at two and five ninths miles an hour, making the one-decibel 'fwoo' with his feet on the seventh-of-an-inch pile of the honey roast and summer gold rug, and did an emergency stop. His mind, however, went to its full RPM in outward silence. "No! Daisy has taken hold of the clock movement. She doesn't know what bad luck it brings. I tried telling her, but she laughed. She said something about Oassie Dee, whoever that is." His part-time work as a superhero spared him the feelings of upwardly-mobile innards and leaking skin that Loïs sometimes said she had, but he did have the need to shield his eyes, which he could not help but see through. "How come I see through walls but not whatever I'm looking through them that at?" he thought.

"Are you OK, Clark?" he heard Loïs ask.

"Yes, I'm fine." Dr. House was right; everyone lies, even superheroes. The TV drama was at least a good insight into the mind of a sigh co-path and that Hugh Laurie was a good at doing an American accent.

"You don't seem it," Loïs went on. "What's the matter? You look like me when I'm - ne'mind."

"I'm fine, but Daisy, please put that back where you got it." He spoke slowly.

"It's only a... What is it?" Loïs asked.

"Clock movement, Loïs," Daisy giggled. "Or not. Clark likes it to be clock stationary."

Clark saw Loïs give a tiny smile.

"It's not what it is that I'm bothered about," he said. "It's where it isn't: on the coffee table beside the bean bag she's sitting on-"

"Who's sitting on?" Daisy asked, rather loudly, Clark thought, but he had something bigger on his mind than identities of clock movement disturbers. Why did she always hate being referred to as "she"?

"-on top of the book about origami, exactly three eighths of an inch from the top right-hand corner and its hanging loop to the left."

"What?" Loïs asked. Shirley was looking from Loïs to him to Daisy to Loïs with her mouth open wide.

"Take the tray, Loïs. Thank you." He remembered to say that more often nowadays but still did not know why it was needed. He took the movement from Daisy's hand.

"Why does it matter?" Loïs asked. She was doing that voice she did when Perry was being picky about the position of that green thingy on his desk.

He spoke quietly, whilst lining up the clock movement with the edge of the book. "It matters because it's the only way to stop my dad getting shingles again."

Loïs sprayed her coffee out of her mouth. The other two women were giggling. "Perry's got nothing on you, Clark," said Daisy, laughing harder.

"You two out!" Loïs said quickly and loudly. "Go! Now! Even faster than that." Clark could see the corners of her mouth twitching. Maybe she's like Oassie Dee, too, he thought. The two gigglers had become full-on cacklers. They stumbled to the door and out, slamming it behind them. The could be heard howling their way to the lift.

"Why did you send them away, Loïs?" The twitching had stopped.

"I know them only too well. They had to go."

"Were they late for an appointment?"

"Yes, that's it. They had an appointment."

"They should have been here, anyway, with this knockdown," Clark said.

"Lockdown. Anyway, I've never seen you obsessing like that. What's come over you?"

Clark was unsure of what to say. The truth. Go with the truth. "You know how Perry says I must have 'super powers'?"

"Like how you were the only one in the office that didn't get salmonella at Don's leaving do?"

"Yes."

"And how you didn't get injured when that van hit you and Stacey but she was?"

"Yes."

"And how you out-ran everyone to score that try in the rugby match?"

"Yes. I get embarrassed by the attention I get." He paused.

"Go on; I'm listening." Her speech was soft and low now.

"By acting like Perry, Sam and Kerry do over their desks, I'm trying to look normal."

"Ah, I get it." Loïs was smiling that baffling smile again. "You're putting on OCD as a smokescreen."

"That's it, yes."

"So that's why you always tap your nose three times before you answer the phone on your desk."

"What are you talking about?"

"What do you mean 'What are you talking about?'?" asked Loïs. She had the look on her that was sometimes followed by a detailed analysis of his behaviour. It was the look that sometimes happened at the same time as Perry saying "You're for it now, Buddy." He never said what Buddy was for. Who was this Buddy, anyway? He flopped onto the settee beside Loïs.

"Clark, you tap your nose like this. Once with the left forefinger on the right-hand side, once with the right forefinger on the left-hand side and both thumbs on the same side."

Clark was about to ask for evidence, like when Loïs asked

anyone bringing her a news story, but-

"Not a word! You do." Her Buddy look changed to another smile. "Mind you, it's funny watching you juggle your mobile if it rings when you're holding it."

Loïs' phone tinkled. She took it out of her pocket to look at the WhatsApp message. "Tanya's sent a re-write of that last song."

Clark was thankful for the change of subject. "What's she done with it? Did she fix it?"

"*Let me hold you in my arms*
I'm so stuck in your charms
Ooh ooh ooh I feel like putty
In your hands like Puff Daddy."

"Ouch. It rhymes better than it did," said Clark. "And the lines are the same length now."

"*No more shoving*
It looks like you're about to get some of that old time loving."

"Oh. That one's even longer now."

"She says she's keeping the rest as it is."

"Well, it is her song. You know how the band agreed that whoever started a song should say how it goes, Loïs."

"I know, but someone's got to fit music to it."

Clark lifted his shoulders and let them fall, like he had seen done at times of doubt. "Re-write it to fit better and do something about the dreadful rhymes."

"The last time we did that, she cancelled our gigs. She's a real control freak."

"That's got to be better than a counterfeit control freak."

"Oh, ha ha." Loïs spoke the words in the way that Clark had learned had something to do with chasms, but he was still trying to work out how gaps in mountains and saying the opposite of what you meant were linked. "Sorry, I forgot you don't make jokes. You were serious."

"I am always serious."

"Hold you hard." Loïs held up her phone towards Clark's head and prodded at the screen. "I want to remember this forever."

"More photographs? OK."

Clark heard his phone give its Adam West Batman ring-tone. He left it a few seconds, before taking it out of his pocket.

Loïs dabbed on her phone. Clark's stopped announcing the superhero. Loïs turned her phone to let him see the video she had shot. "Gotcha!"

***

"What was he playing at? Blood on the white, deep pile carpet!" Diedre snarled, from her end of the Zoom video call. "I don't know how anyone can be that dense. It's astonishing, some of the things he comes out with and does, but that takes first prize. Getting blood on that carpet! It was only a few weeks old, an' all. Most of us would have unwrapped the two steaks over the sink in the kitchen but Clever Clogs Kent chooses to do it in the conference room. Why? It wouldn't have mattered so much if he hadn't dropped them on the carpet when he went tearing off out the room and up the corridor quicker than you could see him. Pillock!"

Loïs spoke up. "To be fair, Diedre, he dashed off to break Tammy's fall when she lost her balance on the stepladder."

"Coincidence. He charged off and was in the right place at the right time."

"No. He seems to have some sixth sense about these things. He's part superhero."

"And a big part dunderhead. Stuperman I'll call him."

"Don't you dare. Shush; he's coming."

Diedre's window shut, and Clark did his carefully choreographed and thoroughly practiced walk from the door to the settee where Loïs was sat with her laptop logged into Zoom with some of their workmates.

"Have you noticed how every superhero is American?" Clark always liked hearing speaker Angharad's strong Welsh accent. He often listened more to the singsonging than to the words. Her trilled "r" was a delight.

"Ah hadn't," answered another Zoomer, a northern English lady. A Georgie, Clark had been told. "Althoo now that Ah think of it, you're raight withoot a doot."

"Wouldn't it be fantastic if an author wrote a story about a European superhero? Get out of the way, Trino. Sorry about my cat walking in front of my webcam. What was I talking about?"

"European superheroes," said Loïs.

"Oh yes, a European superhero story. What do you think, Clark? You're extremely quiet."

Hearing his name brought Clark out of his daydream. "It would be a good investigative journalism story for sure."

Loïs thumped him on the arm, making herself yelp slightly.

"Typical man. You weren't listening, were you?" Angharad said, sounding like Loïs when she was telling him that he had been socially clumsy, but with another accent. Trino jumped onto Angharad's shoulder, blocking her eyes with his fluffy tail. She moved it aside but let him settle where he was.

"I was listening to every note you were singing," Clark said.

"What?" said four women's voices at the same time, allowing for the time-lag over the Internet.

"Saying. Every note you were saying. Word."

Loïs took on the next bit of Clark's social training. "Angharad was talking about having a story with a superhero based here, in Europe. What do you think? Maybe a British Superman?"

"Oh… I doubt it would work. Nobody would take it seriously."

"I think they would," said a new voice. "I'm Bob, Angharad's lodger. I'll see if I can put it into my homework for my creative writing class."

"What a fantastic idea," Angharad almost sang. "Why not put some of your surrealism into it?"

"There's an idea!" Bob sounded like he had won a prize. "I'll give him one or two nervous tics."

Clark did not understand. "Why would a superhero be infested with shy parasites?"

"Sometimes, Clark sweetheart," Loïs spoke like she sometimes did to her five-year-old niece, "I don't think you're entirely human."

***

Clark walked up the street towards the flat, careful not to step on anything that he should not. The gig bag on his back made a soft thump every time his legs hit it. He had not had a clue what Loïs had meant by 'gig bag', at first. He now knew it to be like a rucksack for guitars. It was not a woman that goes to concerts, as Angharad had thought. Silly girl. He played back the shopping trip an hour before to buy the bag and the guitar in it.

He had gone to London's Denmark Street a few miles away from the flat to buy the guitar Loïs had said that she wanted. Music shop on Denmark Street. That was easy enough. He had gone into the shop on the corner of the street, brushing his elbow against the door frame, at the right angle. Musical instruments everywhere. He had gone to the counter. "I've come to buy an electric guitar for my girlfriend," he had said.

"That's lovely of you, but you would be better off going to Rock Lobster two doors down," the saleswoman had told him.

"Why?"

"We only sell orchestral instruments."

"There's a difference?" Clark had seen Yngvie Malmsteen on YouTube playing a Strat with an orchestra. He had told her that, but there was still a difference between electric guitars and orchestras.

Having gone to Rock Lobster, he had made a quick scan of the walls of electric guitars - seeing that the Jaco Patorius signature bass needed its truss rod tightening by two-thirds of a turn - and at the amps on the platform in the middle of the floor. This was the right shop. One of them was the same as the amp that Loïs had. He said to the girl that had been cleaning a guitar, "I have come to buy an electric guitar for my girlfriend."

"Offend 'er?" a man had asked.

"No, she wants one."

"You two have been listening to Tim Vine," the girl had said.

"Yes," the man had said. He had been playing something that sounded like the flute solo to Knights in White Sat In on a bright red Charvel.

Clark had said, "Does he sell guitars?"

The girl had looked up at the ceiling for a third of a second. "He's a comedian. One of his jokes. A Fender - offend her."

"I see. The one she wants is a PRS with free padded gig bag."

"Ah, she was in here yesterday. It's over here. PRS 2020 Custom. Nice."

Clark had followed her to the guitar in question and looked at the name. "It says Paul Reed Smith on it."

"That's right. P - R - S."

Loïs was going to smile at him the way she does, when he told her. For now, though, two tastefully-clothed women were walking towards him, holding a cake box each. Drawing near to him, they smiled. That was nice. He smiled back. They lifted the box lids. He had enough time to see the thick layer of whipped cream on each cake before both of them squelched into his face, one on each side. Not again, he thought. He looked through his creamed-up glasses to watch the two women running back the way that they had come.

"Hey Dinna," he heard one pant, "You do know we custard pied Superman."

"No way! Cool," said the other.

"How the…?" Clark murmured. "Oh yeah."

***

"This is a volcano in full-blooded roar. I'm standing as near as the authorities here will let me. The sound waves coming off it would drown out any pop concert, or should I say 'rock concert'? Spurts of red-hot lava are spewing into the air. A river of molten stone is flowing down the east side. Trees are bursting into flame within seconds of it reaching them. This must be what the citizens of Pompeii saw, minutes before being engulfed in searing agony. Smoke is pouring upwards, high into the sky. This surely is a no-fly zone for aircraft.

"Oh my word. What's that? Lightning bolts inside the smoke stack. Wow! I've not seen anything like this. What a lightshow this would add to our concert. Flash after flash scorches the already superheated air.

"Uh-oh. The lava flow is headed towards us. Gotta go. Clark Kent, BBC Look East."

Anything and everything
Has the potential to be the Cause of grief.
Even love.

Diane Pilbro

How The Drum Helps

The drum has been an essential part of my life for about three years. When, as a beginner, I was amazed that in a circle, all drummers would mirror each other, as if some innate ability to auto connect. Respect was a major issue. Learn from those who knew.

Time arrived when I needed to purchase my own. A special process indeed. I had my sights on a partly carved hollow vessel of exquisitely toned wood from Mali; with reptilian-looking bark that had been smoothed with love and care. I could customise the finish. But, no, realistically I couldn't afford it. I wanted it; adorned with blue ropes caressing its upper torso.

The following lesson, I looked up. A djembe seemed to call to me. Pure serendipity that we met. Placed in the studio, I began to play. It was mine. Made for me. A new relationship pollinated by cohort actions of care.

Gina came through. "Wow, I thought it was Mario playing," she said enthusiastically.

I played with a skill I knew not, or rather it played for me. Owning me and becoming part of my existence. Possessing my spirit, becoming an ethereal spirit coerced by a force stronger than that of my own will; powerful, helping me to achieve my goals. The adhered ropes, freshens, when I feel depleted – a lemon and lime colour of zest and vitality.

Sometimes, the rhythm creates a tsunami, vast, all encompassing beat. It clears, refocuses the mind. Veins pulsate with the beat, defusing frustration. When playing heat is generated, but can cool an emotion to meditate, or excites into a frenetic frenzy.

Throughout the world, drums are used in most countries, for festivals, dancing, religious reasons and cultural diversities. Drums took configuration of a hollow vessel with animal hides on top around the eighth century. Earlier hides were rarely prepared for longevity, as they are today. However, in early war, drums were made from the skin of rival humans. Barbaric, but to the tribal mind was an effective way to overcome ones enemy through empathic magic, literally pounding the power out of them.

Ultimately, the drum, if one allows it, can rejuvenate; sublimely communicating with the emotions, intellect on a conscious and subconscious level. A phenomenon that can enhance ones life, enabling the drummer to stretch beyond their limits. It's grounding. A true drummer should always be humble, knowing that they're always practising their technique and art, to achieve a higher dimension of the self.

A unique language of its own,
Velvet voices merging
Tone licking oxygen and the breath,
Exotic energy of life
Immortal rhythm that, shall still be alive,
When mere mortals fade
Memory, echoes an acoustic paradigm of ecstasy.

Cloud Calypso

Laying on the cool glass. Sunbeams dance on my eyelids. Shoulders digging into the ground. I could imagine, if I stood up, there would be an imprint of my body in the earth. I looked up, clouds gently drifting on the breeze. Many shapes, contours, textures and shades of white. I transcend. I enter one. Heavy, ladened with precipitation. I bathe in the pure water droplets and bask in ice crystals Not knowing when it would open and cast its innards onto the land. It would fill the indentation of my body. I would be a reflection. I would become a body puddle. My form being filled with water. Sun reflecting onto the imprint of my shoulders, making them light and free. I would be absorbed into the ground; become part of the earth.

Here I am floating in this cloud; low level cloud, cumulus, lying below 6.500ft. This new existence is beautiful, drifting so high in the breeze. My body is one with this cloud moisture. Gently caressing my heavy shoulders. They float, no longer heavy.

My head is light - spinning gently. Body weightless in this heavy cloud, that could weigh more than 1 million pounds. Where would it take me? When would it disperse?

If its formation went through metamorphosis, could it become altocumulus, forming between 6,500 and 20,000 feet? This is my home now. Happy to give up my worldly existence and be part of this ethereal realm. Sublime and free as this was really meant for me. I'm floating. Totally at one. At last I've found my destiny. No other place I'd rather be. The cliché says: 'every cloud has a silver lining'. But this cloud is not just a silver lining. Because silver and gold are just mere metals. Precious maybe. Up here, wealth means nothing. Magical nature and phenomenon paramount.

I'm intoxicated, drunk with the pure sheer amount of water. Body being made up of 99% atoms and up to 60% water. Perfect. I'm intoxicated. So what better place for my body, soul, mind, spirit and shoulders; that were heavy, now are vapours.

Intoxicated and totally immersed now. I've given up my bodily form. I've become a cloud. Everywhere is open. This cloud has let me in, welcoming. No doors or windows. No feeling of claustrophobia. Cloud chariot shall take me anywhere I'd like to go. This is my journey, with no real destination as I've given myself to the cloud.

Now, I the cloud, is greeted by a mountain. It could be the Himalayas. Could be 3.40am. A special time in the morning when souls meet in meditation. What would happen to me. I'd forgotten, I AM the cloud. I am taken by the mountain; now in control. I disperse. My contents dance droplets all over the mountain. I can't imagine a better place to be; timeless mountains with forests underneath. I can rest now. As I rain, I rain down, rain down now, I rain down. Getting faster, I rain down. I'm released. Rain down now, I'm released. I rain. Rain. I'm released. And, now in equilibrium, we reign in this terrain. Mountain with texture and colour strong, glistens in the sun, reflecting on the cloud's body puddle. Inner consciousness sacred.

Harmony rules.

Silver Birch

The ageless woman lives in the countryside, near an old cemetery. Locals call her Silver Birch. Era timeless. Candlelight dances in her quiet window. Door always open. She fears nothing.

Silver Birch reads the signs from the natural world and receives messages from the creatures. Silver Birch, bringing new beginnings and a powerful healer for those unwell.

She looks to the eagle for freedom.

Hawk to be observant; to see messages in the environment and to stay alert.

Deer, for gentleness; to connect to minds and hearts.

Let the stillness and determination of snowy owl take Silver Birch beyond.

At night, she transcends into a realm of pure white light, as she gently chants,

"Bonne nuit, dorm bien. Je pense à toi."

***

Nicholas, a horrid, arrogant man lived in the small village. His child had fever. He was worried, but still continued to ignore the locals, obstinate and offensive. Sarcastic, to a person at the diary, asking for milk. Silver Birch came in and sensed the atmosphere.

"Why sir, this perplexity?" she asked gently.

"Don't interfere wild woman."

She ignored this comment and simply said, "I can help your child."

"How do you know? You crazy woman. No one knows," he said aggressively.

"Think sir, before you speak, I am here. It is your choice whether to take my help."

He abruptly turned around, walking out. His bright, red jacket, a flash, as he left the door.

"What an obstinate man," said the dairy maid.

"He needs to learn, to be patient, then his children will not suffer," replied Sliver Birch.

Smiling politely, she left to return to her peaceful sanctuary. Thinking of the fevered child.

As she walked along the road, she passed the man. Face as white as his coat was red. Five children greeted him near the garden. His hostility scared them, but they still showed their devotion.

Silver Birch, felt their pain, but detached herself from their negative emotion. Thought deeply how she could help them. Wondered how the man would accept, or if he'd allow the fevered child to continue to feel unwell.

Anger grew in Silver Birch, an emotion she rarely felt. She was going the help the child despite this situation. She would find the mother, offer her remedies from the forest. If the mother accepted, the child would be calmed and return to a state of health. But, the future, would depend on the attitude of the man. He would have to change. Allow his children to live more peaceful, less frenetic lives.

Days passed. Silver Birch, spent her time meditating on thoughts, healing her inner turmoil, at present was manifesting. This was all wrong. Action had to be taken.

For solace, she went to the forest. Immediately at one with the trees and pure sky. The swaying of the branches soothed her, the breezed kissed her gently giving her the answers. Birds singing a beautiful dawn chorus. Their melody too offering hope. She found the correct leaves, their colour exquisite, texture and moisture too was perfect. Gathering these in her hands, She praised the forest and left.

As she approached the house of the frenetic family, screams and shrieks echoed though the ether. Her ears alarmed, her nerves shaking. She knocked the door.

A woman appeared. The nature of the woman didn't look friendly, her eyes a beautiful but cold blue. Silver Birch stood her ground.

"I come with help for the fever of your child, if you allow it," she said, offering a small parcel, which the woman didn't accept.

"My husband is not in. I wish you to see my child," she said tentatively.

"Thank you." No further words were exchanged, as Silver Birch entered the house, with a little trepidation, but with the gentleness of deer.

Passing through the dank, cold house, she found the fevered child. Again no words spoken. The mind created the language. Placing the moist leaves upon the child's forehead, she turned to the woman.

"If it's your wish, you should allow the healing of the leaves to soothe until dusk. Remove them, and you child will recover. But take heed, your husband should relearn, to allow some equilibrium to the household. So all can breathe, rest, play and most importantly sleep." With that, she smiled at the child, who's blank face gazed back.

Silver Birch returned to her home. Anticipating the outcome. She would not spend long with this though, knowing she could not predict. This being beyond her powers. So happily, played with her cat, who was watching the birds in the trees. Not interested in the instinct of the feline. They were in harmony today.

The next morning. A knock was at her door. Of course, Silver Birch, whose door is always open, simply said "Enter." She feared not.

In walked the man, Nicholas. His face appeared calmer, less antagonistic or fierce.

"My child is brighter today. I shall bring you your milk everyday from now on," he said.

Brendan Pearson

Howard Flinch – an Introvert in a State of Angst (excerpt)

This is an excerpt from "Howard Flinch – an Introvert in a State of Angst" published by Chipmunka publishing (2007) under Brendan's pseudonym, Brendan Reason.
In this excerpt, Santa, a central character of the novel and loosely autobiographical, has just been discharged from St Muggs psychiatric unit.

Carol Cushion sat on a hard plastic chair in the empty Gippeswyk drama studio. The inside of the building was completely blacked out. Seats were on raised steps to give a good view of the stage at the far end. On the stage were two large dustbins, both back stage left and an armchair, centre front stage. Centregroup, a top-class amateur drama group were putting on Endgame by Samuel Beckett at the Drama Studio for three nights. In an hour's time the final performance was to take place.

Santa entered the studio. "Is Sue coming to the play tonight?" he asked Carol. "She said she might," Carol replied.

Sue was a student occupational therapist from a college in London on placement at St Muggs. During OT sessions, Sue would gaze at Santa fondly, or so it seemed to him, through well made up cow eyes and talk to him in a kindly way. Once during a therapy session she had chosen to sit next to him and work with him. The next day he painted a picture of a vase, full of green flowers, with her face on it. Santa had the Hots, capital H, for her. A Titanic desolation was to follow with her return to her London college.

Breaking into his reverie about Sue, other members of Centregroup began to arrive at the studio. Mick Marlowe the director of Endgame; David Shakespeare who played the part of Hamm - the man who cannot stand up; and Dan Bacon who played Clove - the man who cannot sit down. Lisa Snuggle played the part of Nell who was confined to a dustbin and Santa who played Nagg, Nell's husband, who occupied the other dustbin. Like all Beckett plays the outlook was rather bleak but Santa found Endgame strangely beautiful and was glad to be in it. In truth he longed for greater roles, but a small but significant role like that of Nag was about his limit at that time. In the cramped space of the dustbin he shook with tension as he delivered his lines.

He enjoyed the social compensations of belonging to a well known drama group without the stress of taking on more demanding roles. There were parties after productions, during production and before productions. The group loved the songs he wrote and sang – particularly Valentines Blues – an improvised song about receiving nothing but tax demands on Valentines day. On one occasion an ex-member of Scaffold, John Gorman, and his group were performing at the Studio and asked if anyone wanted to do a turn. Santa was first to respond guitar in hand and ran through five of his songs to enthusiastic applause. Afterwards John Gorman took his contact details.

There were darker days in Santa's life. Following his stay at St Muggs he continued to experience extreme mood swings that were debilitating. Having a good friend like Carol Cushion, who was also an occupational therapist, helped him through many black moods. When Santa was in a state of despair he would go on longs walks to work out how to stop feeling so awful. During these excursions he would generally create a mental exercise to do, like repeating the phrase – 'think of nothing' - which struck him as very Beckett. The exercise kept him happy for a few days. Then dark thoughts would inevitably return; thoughts of the things that he longed for in his life– sometimes desperately so, but seemed always beyond his reach. Then the thought perhaps he didn't deserve those things, Then the thought that he was a failure at life. Then the thought… and so on, leading into darker and darker realms of his psyche.

Sometimes he felt unable to continue and again the thoughts of Samuel Beckett came to mind : "you must go on; I can't go on; I'll go on."

Warmth

Wood smoke
Down the dirt track.
The fire
Cracks the dry wood.
It burns bright
In kind eyes

At Dark Times

There are times when my joys
- The joys of this great world -
They crumble down to dust.
The light of the day it fades
And music just seems to drone.
A sharp needle unthreads
My soul until the words
Of my lady are lost

Debbie

Red shades of brown
Shine setting sun
Of woman's hair.

You pull on your coat
- jumble splendid -
And start to run.

You drop your haste
and walk – a girl
with a golden crown.

The Girl Next Door

Friendly as roses
that burn in the summer,
She lets you take her
To the flower of the night
Where no stars shine
but still she brings light.

Once through her garden
I went my lonely way
To find I was lost,
Surrounded by flowers,
Drowned in their perfume,
A drugged bee I lay.

Since then I have not left
That deep summer night,
That winding way,
That dark weed tangle
That might lead nowhere
But tells me to stay.

In fond memory of Brendan Pearson – a true creative and stalwart member of Inside Out Community.
These poems are from Brendan's collection, Fragments of Eve.
Published by kind permission of his family.

Algae forms on the pond surface,
Summer sleeping.

Mai Black

To a Raindrop

Too fat for the cloud
You fell downwards
Learning gravity
And wind patterns
And vectors
And quadratics
You flew faster than starlings
Soared swifter than seagulls

Dreaming of deserts
And parched places
Of snowy pines
And tall fruit trees

Spinning in sunlight
Splitting the light
Into emerald-sapphire
And bright crimson-amethyst

To fall so far
To hit only

A glass
Invisible barrier
Locked fast against you

But you, bubble on my window
Fleck on my glassy plane
Will return to the clouds
Be born once more

Maybe next time
A rainforest

Reflections

alone in the library café
joined by a couple
and a tiny brown-eyed baby

—a call on her mobile
a frantic goodbye

I am left with three full teacups
feeling empty
Wandering
The long night is broken
across the horizon
the trees and the houses
and cathedral spire crosses
are moulded pink putty
a sleep sunken city
of rain dripping gutters
and chestnut tree splatters
will her steps dare echo
as the sun finds her shadow
on the leaf littered pavement
and the concrete embankment
past the eyeless stone lions
to the unpeopled bridges
to a pale-yellow window
she tries to call home

An ancient hillock.
The tree of life,
Reflections of the sky.

Sallyanne Webb

Haven

Here in this hidden cove
sheltered between rocky mottled cliffs,
the tick of the clock is silenced and stilled
and a salty breeze unfurls my brow – for a while.
My toes curl into soft golden sand,
gulls hover and land on rich pickings
and despair releases its grip on me – for a while.

Here in this treasure trove
the sun glistens on a sapphire sea
like a thousand sparkling diamonds
and razor-edged words are shaved – for a while.
A boat chugs to the opposite shore
where folklore brings smugglers to life
and the tide swallows the bile of yesteryear – and I smile.

Portrait of Me

I see I am long in the face and long in the tooth
and your lacy truth flutters in the air
as you stare into my eyes,
blue/green watery pools that I wish were turquoise or teal
but feel like the sludge of the North Sea.

I see sturdy under-eye bags
carrying doubt, cries and rage
as you flick through the pages of my story,
some open, some kept on a shelf behind the door.

I see I am thin lipped, tight lipped,
from the dawn of my days
I learned to zip it and became a cripple
before a step was taken.

I see shadows cast down through the years,
shades I pulled down to hide the fears of the monster
under my bed, muzzled yet breathing.

I see blemishes and patches and dot-to-dot spots
and rough skin bearing the imprint of uninvited hands
and bands of pain woven with shame.

I see a face
plain, ordinary, forgettable -
yet I have not forgotten.

Solitary Existence

In the neighbourhood of widows hearts,
maiden aunts,
the poor orphan darling,
she may
settle gloomily into doom,
arrange dreary frills,
be a picture of a petted past
and be very nice indeed.

Or she may
shoot the fire in winter,
scatter scandal through defiance,
knot smoke in circles
and bathe in crazy catastrophe.

Be your own reward.

(*found poetry from 'Live Alone and Like It' by Marjorie Hillis*)

Crocus grow
Like a carpet purple of tears.

Peter Watkins

The Mystery of Coopers Hollow

After that nothing grew there.
Assorted scientists visited but no explanation could be found.
Gradually the area of decay spread,
until the whole wood and
the fields beyond were dead.

And there was no sound.

Eventually it reached the first houses,
officials assured, no one would come to any harm.
Rumours spread. Climate change, nuclear rain
toxic waste, ecocide,
all were said to be to blame.

And there was growing alarm

A bleakness of spirit invaded us, those that stayed,
leaving us as joyless as the lifeless land.
God knows how we survived that festering sadness
The haunting sleepless dreams
the collective madness.

Then there was the small skeletal hand.

The silted pond was dredged for what remained -
a bike, a bracelet, a shoe,
all hers it seems, were reclaimed,
confirming what at the time we could not contemplate,
missing seemed a kinder fate.

And suspicions grew

Sometime later he was found hanging from a dead tree.
A confessional note of deep remorse and fear
pinned there for all to see.
Still we struggle to accept the facts that
a face we knew could mask such evil acts.

And the bluebells grew again that year

Billy Wizz

Like all good strikers, Billy Wizz Williams had anticipation, a kind of intuition about the way a move would develop or a pass would be played. He had a sixth sense about where he needed to be to receive the ball and create a scoring opportunity. Wizz by name and by nature – he was fast, a reputation that attracted the attentions of the 'cloggers' of the game. Despite being a marked man , most games he rode or side-stepped the tackles, always having a cheeky smile for his adversaries. In his first five seasons in the third tier of the professional leagues his goal tally had been prodigious: Fourteen during the first season, twenty the second season; twenty two the third; twenty three the fourth; and sixteen during the final injury-hit season. The injury was serious, it was not one he would fully recover from; few footballers came back from a torn cruciate ligament. He bore no grudge against Bovine Butler, the infamous bull of the Rangers back four. It was not a dangerous tackle, just hard; Billy's studs had kept him anchored, while his knee twisted on impact. At twenty-two, with Premier League clubs sniffing and a potential international career ahead of him, his life as a footballer was suddenly over.

There was now a void where his life had been. What had been bright with promise was now dull and empty. The support of his girlfriend, friends and family had been unwavering, yet the stone in his heart could not be rolled away with kind words and hopeful platitudes. His thoughts that day on the moor above the town were arrows of dejection, any fortitude he had crumbled.

He set off along the old pilgrimage route that crossed the moor. The path was seventy-eight miles long ending at a ruined abbey on the East coast. In summer this was a popular walk but as autumn shaded into winter few other walkers were up there. He had not intended to go far but something impelled him to continue. He walked briskly, at times almost running as if he could walk away from the anguish that had engulfed his life. He was wearing a weatherproof coat and boots but had no food or water. He walked all day without seeing anyone until light began to fade and the next marker post became more difficult to identify. He was tired and it had begun to rain. There were no guiding lights offering a direction in which to head. He felt in his pockets for his mobile, simultaneously remembering changing coats before he left the house. Billy's sense of desolation deepened. Nearby a limestone outcrop offered some shelter. There he squatted, body curled in a foetal position, hood up, back against the rock, its solidity offering some strange comfort.

In the morning he woke to the excited barking of a terrier. Apprehensively two boys, who must have been eight or nine years old, stood further back, staring. As he lifted his head and then stiffly clambered to his feet, the boys, wide eyed now, moved closer.

"You're Billy Wizz aren't you," said the first boy.

"They said you were missing on the news last night," said the second.

"I got a bit lost," was all Billy could answer.

"Could I have your autograph," said the first boy.

"Me too please," said the second, offering a ballpoint and a forearm.

"Sure thing," said Billy, "where is the nearest village?"

"Just a mile down that path," said the first boy pointing, "do you want to walk back with us?"

"Sure thing," said Billy.

"You're still my favourite footballer," said the first boy.

"Mine too," said the second, who unselfconsciously had slipped his hand into Billy's as they walked.

The Room

One, two, three strides. He stops. He turns. One, two, three strides. Stops. Turns. Three more strides. Stops. Turns. Each short stride is a metre. Each length is three metres. Ten lengths, thirty metres. One hundred lengths, three hundred metres. A thousand lengths, three thousand metres. He can walk six thousand metres at a time. Walking three times a day he walks eighteen kilometres, about eleven miles. One, two, three strides. Stops. Turns. One, two, three strides. Stops. Turns. Doesn't allow himself to think of the futility. He keeps walking. He walks on. Three more strides. Stop. Can't stop. He walks. How long have I been here he thinks. Checks the marks on the wall. Ten days. Forget the first two days, then he paced aimlessly. He has travelled one hundred and forty four kilometres, around 89 miles. What's the point. Is there a point. Yes there is a point.

A rest. An interval. He sits. He drinks. He drinks one third of his daily water ration.

He observes the room. It is locked. Is it locked. Yes it's locked. It is shuttered. A filament of light shows between the joins. It's bare, It's drab. It's inhospitable. A bed. A chair. A basin. A bucket. It smells of excrement. It smells of fear.

The room observes him. He walks. He stops. He looks about. He walks. He listens. He murmurs. What does he murmur. Is he losing his mind. Is he saving his mind. He stops. He walks. What good does it do. Why does he not give up. Why does he not despair.

He begins again. Three strides. Stop. Turn. Walk. Three more strides. Stop. Turn. Stops. Looks. Here the path keeps to the valley floor. To the left the familiar snow capped peaks. On the right the river flowing fast from the snow melt, hurrying toward the sea. Soon he will reach the pass. Maybe not today. Tomorrow perhaps. Before that the village. He will stay there the night. Before the climb. Beyond the pass, the forest. Beyond the forest, the plain. Beyond the plain, home.

Just a day
That frames a life.
Fate and chance.

Maggie Singleton

Christmas Rose (or, Allowed)

This story is set in the days before Christmas. It is improbably snowy. In Middle England. The pandemic we knew as Covid 19 rolls on.

***

Rose wondered if her boots were leaking, her feet were so very cold. As was her face.

"It'll be all over by Christmas," he'd said. She had heard that lie before, long ago. Something her mother had said. About a war.

Why was it that she trudged this old path every day? On her own. Leaving her warm kitchen for her daily constitutional. Allowed out – that was it – for essential shopping and exercise, and other things that she didn't qualify for, like going to work or going to school. She couldn't remember the whole list of what was allowed. Or not.

It had become a habit, the trudge, she supposed.

And this snow! Well! She hadn't seen the like of it in years. Not in December. She vividly remembered most of the snowy Christmases of her life. Not that many in her 80 years.

Even though she forgot the names of the people on the telly who told her what was allowed. Or not.

Trudge, thought Rose aloud. She rolled the word around in her mouth. An interesting word. Onamata-whatsit. Sounded like the sound of her boots in the snow. Trudge, trudge. Rose chuckled.

It had been months and months now, this lock up, lock in, lock down. Staying in. To stay well. No choir. No singing with her friends. No WI. No knit and natter. Empty days. Bloody telly.

“She's good for her age isn’t she? I say, you’re good for your age.”

Oh please, thought Rose. Whatever does that mean. I’m neither deaf nor stupid. She didn’t say it aloud. Mind you, she had left the small gas ring on for an hour this morning after she made her porridge. Warmed up the kitchen nicely. Porridge was good too. Rose chuckled aloud again.

Trudge, trudge. Dark now. Only four o'clock. No-one much about. Stay home, stay well. Bloody virus. Let it out , thought Rose, into the snow. The cold'll kill it off.

Rose trudged along the path by the churchyard wall. The snow was thicker here, where it had drifted against the wall, white icing edges on the flints.

She looked over the wall across the churchyard. Quiet as the grave. Rose chuckled aloud again. No offence intended.

Then she heard it. Quiet at first. The organ. Couldn’t be. The church was closed again. No services. No singing. Not allowed.

There – again! God Rest Ye Merry Gentlemen. She strained to hear. Definitely the Organ. Not the piano. Rose turned under the Lychgate and pushed the old wooden gate open against the resistant snow. The path to the porch caught the sulphurous light from a street lamp on the corner of St Mary’s Lane and Bridge Street.

I wonder if the river is frozen over. In the distance Rose thought she heard her brother's voice calling out. “Don’t be daft Rose, it’s not strong enough to take your weight. If you fall in you'll freeze to death in five seconds. Mum'll be furious. We'll get no tea." She crossed the river quite safely. Slipping and sliding. When Roger followed, the ice cracked alarmingly and he retreated.

"Meet you at the bridge," she called, laughing. It was not often she got one over on him. She missed him. And her mum.

There again, the sound of the merry organ drifted towards her. The path was pristine. Glistening snow. Shame to spoil it really, but Rose was drawn by the music. She had missed it so. The church, the friendship, the singing. Her little choir.

Of course, some of her friends, (and some who weren't her friends), had kept in touch. On the phone. Cramming in calls when it was free. Fetching shopping. But they had little interesting conversation. No-one had been anywhere. Done anything.

"How's work?" she asked her son.

"Nightmare!" the usual reply. "My back is killing me."

Not the virus though, she didn't say aloud, killing you.

"Stuck on the laptop all day. Kids driving me nuts now school's closed."

"How are the children?" she asked.

"Bored. Avoiding doing the work the school has set. Desperate to go out in the snow."

Not allowed. Stay home, stay well.

"Hello Grandma. We miss you."

Rose felt a tear roll from her eye and freeze on her cheek. She swallowed.

"They need to stay away, Mum. To keep you safe."

Rose thought she would swap a drop of virus for a hug and a cuddle. A game of scrabble round the warm kitchen table. Steaming mugs of cocoa and digestives.

Rose realised she'd been standing still. Her feet were so cold she couldn't really feel them. She stamped and trudged forward into the deepening white. Towards the door of St Mary's.

There was a glow from the window by the porch. Flickering. The organ had started up again clearer now, and she could hear the voices. Wobbly voices like her own these days. Oh Little Town…

A moment of annoyance. Was the choir meeting again. Without her? Surely not. It wasn't allowed.

Rose had been a chorister at St Mary's since Sunday School. Trilling along with her friends. Girls allowed. Where had she heard that before? There weren't enough boys to make a decent sound in the cavernous church, so the vicar had allowed a mixed choir. Reverend Roberts. Dead now of course. Now they had Reverend Wilson. Sonia. Rose couldn't quite get her brain around that. Not in real life. She'd loved the Vicar of Dibley. Dawn. Geraldine. Oh that Telly Tubby wedding! And of course Rose knew that women were just as good as men at everything – better mostly, but somehow Rev'd Sonia… – well, now it was allowed.

"She's nice enough. Lovely girl. Good teeth. But a bit more gravitas required I think," Rose confided to her son.

Still fighting the men though, aren't we, thought Rose. Not equal unless they allow it. Long way to go yet. But in the choir, equality ruled. She loved it, choir practice. Tea in the church afterwards. Practice at home. Services and weddings. The church fete. Funerals. Sonia encouraged them to sing everywhere. She had even organised them a slot at a folk festival. Rose expected hippies – well there were, but all older than she remembered. There were youngsters too. Loud. A bit drunk on local beer she thought. Sunburnt. Jumping and gyrating in front of the outdoor stage. The real hippies cheered and clapped from their festival chairs, sipping tea from flask cups. Perhaps it was gin! The choir had sung Strawberry Fayre, opening their set. The old hippies all joined in. The ladies of the choir wore summer frocks. Some of the men wore baggy shorts and sandals. Imagine! Rose bought a garland of silk flowers for her hair from one of the stalls. Seemed just right on the day, but her grandson said she looked like a bridesmaid. A bridesmaid! Rose had never been a bridesmaid. Only a bride. Just the once.

Rose reached the heavy oak door of the church. The stone

slabs of the porch were dusted with blown snow - no footprints though. Rose stamped her feet to get the worst of the snow from her boots. It occurred to her for the first time that they must've been there for some time to have left no smudges in the icing sugar in the porch or footprints in the deep and crisp and even.

The door opened at the lightest pressure of her gloved hand resting in the iron ring. No creak. No effort. Swung open.

The voices of the choir filled her senses. Rose stepped down into the church. She closed her eyes, smelt the warm musty familiar smell, breathed in the candle smoke, and began to sing her part of In The Bleak Mid Winter. As she turned slowly, instinctively, towards the alter and the choir stalls, opening her eyes, expecting to see the shining Christmas church, the music faded, the voices thinned and evaporated. The warmth turned to chill, the only light from the candles on the advent crown at the head of the nave, one remaining unlit.

Rose walked carefully along the nave towards the lights. It was so quiet now. All sound muffled by the snow and the thick stone walls of St Mary's. She took a taper, and gently lit the final candle on the top of the crown, bobbing a prayer towards the statue of the Virgin in her niche in the wall. She pulled her coat closer round her against the still cold.

"Hello Rose," said Sonia, "I'm so glad you came. It doesn't seem right, an empty church on Christmas Eve. I'm so pleased to see you. Shall I put the kettle on in the vestry. There might be some digestives. Mind you, I'm not sure it's allowed."

Esme Pears

The Bears

A prose poem

I love the bears: the moving, grating of their jaws, the rhinos with their horns of silver and the interplay of the shadows, the way the darkness falls, and the bears keep running and the wildness and the fury and the animal instinct overtakes. There is a magic in the shapes where the shadows of the future meet the shadows of the past and the movement speaks of the growth of humankind, the way we hope and keep hoping, and the bears. The bears and wolves and wild beasts that came from the darkness and leave into more of the same, I would dance like a horse or bare my soul and pretend I didn't exist. I would be a miracle.

A Death in Reverse

He tells me everything will be okay because he loves me –
nothing could trump that.
He holds my hand.
Slowly, my tears stop falling.
I begin to cry the moment I see his face appear around the
corner; he is here, though I desperately tried not to be.
Never mind, my paper is wet with tears – unreadable.
My sentence should end sorry, I forget that.
I write I am *so, so, so, so, so, so, so, so, so* until *so* isn't a word
anymore.
I cannot see to read when a text beeps through on my phone.
I feel so alone, nothing makes sense here and I don't
understand why.
I wake up in a bed that is not my own – in a body that is not
mine either.
It goes dark.
The room is white, and the windows are high; the light that
floods in is artificial.
I try to cling on to the space about me.
There are voices now, loud in my head: *stay with us, tell us
your name, stay with us love.*
I am rolled from one bed to another – nothing about this is
dignified.
That is all I remember.
There are men in my house.
I can't remember whether I took them all.
I shovel the pills into my mouth, gulping down mouthfuls of
water in between.
In my room, sat up in my bed, I line up all the tablets I have
saved - stuffed into pockets and hidden in jars – just for this
purpose.
I am going to die.

The Puppeteer

I conduct them into the room and let the door shut firmly behind them. Her parents are tense with the strain of holding space in outstretched arms. They sense my presence, but I am unseen by all but the girl. As they perch on the edges of their seats, I lounge in my familiar space in front of the door.

"So, how has it been since I last saw you?"

I glance at the girl who simply shrugs as her parents both speak at once, their words tangling, chasing each other, catching up then backing off. Already the girl is scoring the back of her left thumb with her right thumb nail, repeating the motion until it forms deep, angry, red scratches which ooze blood and make her father frown. He bites back his words, and I smile with satisfaction.

The psychiatrist turns on his chair to face the girl, her gaze is fixed resolutely on the floor, on the blue carpet tiles with their dubious-looking stains. Her face is reddening as all the eyes in the room turn towards her. I allow myself to tut by her right ear.

"Cat got your tongue?"

Then the psychiatrist speaks her name, injecting a gravity into the vowels of it so there is no mistaking that he intends to gain a response from her. I know I am safe though – she has lifted her head but only to stare at the unorganised jumble of books and papers on the desk behind his chair. Silence holds the room almost as tightly as I, as everyone waits for her to speak.

"How do you feel at the moment? Do you think things are getting any better?"

The girl frowns and glances into her lap. A hole has begun to form in the cuff of her oversized jumper, and she plucks at it. She knows what she wants to say; but she also knows that the question is not directed at her: it is for me, and I will never answer. No one can make me.

The psychiatrist tries again "How's school at the

moment?"

More silence. We both know this game: the false friendliness, the not-so innocent questions. It is all an attempt to win her trust, though I have ensured she trusts no one. I dominate this stage; the girl is merely my puppet.

"See!" Her father bursts out, just as it seems the room has been conquered. "This is what I find so difficult. I try to talk to her, but she never says anything. How can I help if I don't know what's wrong?"

Momentarily stunned she looks up, eyes wide – the proverbial rabbit caught in the headlights. Her mother reaches out and takes the girl's hand, gently stroking it as she once caressed her baby's forehead when she woke in the night, confused and afraid.

"I'm sorry…" the girl whispers hoarsely.

Perhaps she means it, but I laugh aloud at the prospect that she might believe she could ever atone. I see the doubt shadow her pale face almost immediately.

"You don't have to be sorry. You have nothing to be sorry for. You just have to get better…"

"You just have to get better," her mother repeats quietly – already as certain of her failure as I am of my success.

The girl's guilt is written plainly across her thin, white face. I feel myself swell as her eyes flicker between the door and the window and she concludes there is no way out. She says nothing to her mother, knowing as well as I that whatever she might say would be a lie. I am the puppeteer, and what I would say is not what they want to hear, so she keeps her mouth shut. Instead, the girl squeezes her mother's hand: a futile effort to console. Already tears are creeping from the corners of her eyes and she is powerless to stop them.

The psychiatrist takes this moment to change his approach. "I wonder, would it be okay if I spoke to you on your own for a while?"

We all know that this is not really a request at all and that the nod the girl gives is just her part in a predetermined script. All the same, her parents wait for their daughter's permission before they rise from their seats and I move aside to let them out of the room. She watches as they go. It is not until the door shuts behind them and the dull look returns to her eyes that I realise with some amusement that she had dared to hope that *on her own* meant without *me* too. I move away from the door to sit beside her in the seat just abandoned by her mother. The irony is immense.

"I realise that you don't find this easy, so I really appreciate your efforts."

She nods robotically at the psychiatrist in his swivel chair. Her eyes are now fixed on the clock to the right of his head. The second hand moves jerkily around the face – too slowly for her liking, there is still twenty minutes of the session left.

"I wondered whether there was anything you wanted to ask me, perhaps you have some questions about the illness?"

The Illness. I smirk, satisfied with this title, and greatly entertained by the thought that this man could even imagine that he had the answers. Or that she could ever bring herself to ask. She knows that any answers he might give would only be lies and that only this is true: there is no way that she could ever be free from *me*.

We wait in the almost-silence. The clock seems to have stopped and the girl shudders as I squeeze her hand.

Thomas Freestone

Wings, and Other Straws

Light pooled, and so did the rain. Drizzle danced in the wind, while a leaky drainpipe slowly dripped. While children counted the seconds between these drips, the classroom clock ticked onwards to 3:20pm; hometime.

Calls for "storytime" gradually peeled children away from the colouring they were supposed to be doing. Eventually, everyone was more-or-less settled, and the teacher was enthusiastically presenting the book's cover.

"See this bird? Look at how *shiny* his wings are."

This met with a mixed reception. Some kids stared, rapt already, while others were listless. Three boys near the back were still focused on the leaky drainpipe, until the Teaching Assistant got them to look towards the front.

Seconds later, she began.

Deep in the woods, there were countless birds.

A customary pause, for everyone to admire the illustrations.

Some birds danced, others made art.
But all birds, young and old, large and small, sang.
They sang together, from sunrise to sunset… to sunrise again!
Each and every bird in harmony.
Until, one day, they didn't.

One day a beautiful bird, with shining wings, came to the forest.

A pause, for the children to appreciate the two-page spread.

He flew non-stop, day and night.
At first the birds enjoyed this new friend and tried to sing along to his strange song.
But day after day, night after night, he sang.
It seemed the only thing he wanted was for everyone else to gaze at his shimmering wings.
He didn't leave space for any other songs but his own.

Some children gasped theatrically – perhaps more at the teacher's tone than anything. Others simply looked confused. One boy, somewhere in the middle, was preoccupied rubbing saliva into his shoes.

But the crafty crows had a plan.
One night, when he'd finally settled into a noisy sleep…

Here she paused again, turning the book to show the shiny "Zzzs".

… the birds of the forest did what they had to.

Swifts darted, crows plucked,
Bird after bird helped them take away each and every shining feather.

The next morning, he woke.
His morning cry turned into sobs, when he saw his plumage gone.

This time, a lot of children leaned in to see the illustration. The shiny bird was now a matte black, with nothing but a shiny outline to remind the readers of what he used to look like.

He scoured the forest, still wailing.
A feather here, woven into a nest.
A feather there, clasped in the beak of a dancer.

"Why?" he cried, "what did I do to deserve this?"

"Well," replied a crow, "we did you a favour, really."

"I was just being myself!"

"Perhaps you were. But sing along with us, and you'll become someone ***better****."*

The teacher smiled at the ending. Turned a page and the book. She held it so that the whole class could see the final piece of artwork – soft tawny feathers beginning to grow on the shiny-outlined body.

A boy began to softly sob. She frowned. He yelled and flinched away when the TA tried to put a consoling hand on his shoulder. In a second, disruption reigned once more – so much for settling the kids down before their parents arrived.

Honestly, though. she'd been thinking of recommending that child for the gifted and talented programme next year. Perhaps she shouldn't - after all, he couldn't even recognise a happy ending.

Neurodivergence and Narrative

"Nothing about us without us."

You might have heard these words before, or you might not – I suspect it depends on the circles you move in. It's been used for a great deal of different topics, I believe, but I've seen it most commonly used in the online autistic community. As slogans go, I think it's up there with the greats – catchy, memorable, and delivers the key message in a simple, punchy way. But a slogan is not an argument, despite what some folks in online comment sections might think, and so I intend to dig a little deeper into this slogan today. To make things a little more focused, I'll be using the recent film called Music as my go-to example for why narratives can be so harmful (because, sad to say, the film is stuffed to bursting with such things).

First of all, I think I should say up front that I'm autistic, with a side helping of ADHD. So yes, I'm undoubtably biased here. But at the same time, it's only a reason I want things to get better. Besides, so what if I have a bias for wanting a world where people make more effort to understand others?

But I digress.

So, Music. It's a film (and I use that term charitably) by the singer/songwriter Sia, about an autistic girl called Music (yes, really), and her life. Except it isn't – it's a movie about a recovering alcoholic/drug-dealer called Zu (which genuinely seems to be short for Kazoo) having to learn to care for her autistic half-sister after their grandmother dies. See the problem? If not, let me continue – Zu learning to care for her half-sister leads her to fall in love with her new neighbour, who helps her teach her how to take care of Music (he's played by the amazing Leslie Odom Jr but is himself a dodgy collection of race-related offensive narratives).

So yeah, this movie should have probably been called Kazoo. But really that isn't the core issue. The core issue isn't that a neurotypical dancer was cast as a non-verbal autistic girl. Hell, the core issue isn't even that the film advocates for restraint techniques that have literally killed autistic folks in the past and calls these "crushing [them] with our love," (although that certainly isn't good). Nope, you could cut out those scenes (as Sia has promised to do), and the film would still be an offensive eyesore towards autistic people. Why? Narratives.

We all use narratives in our lives and in the lives of people around us. From things as simple as imagining how a dice will roll based on what it rolled last time, to stories we comfort ourselves with about how we're changing for the better from the setbacks we all face. We need stories to make sense of our lives, just like how our brains dream to help process our emotions, thoughts and memories.

Thing is, we apply these stories to other people too, and that's where the problems can start.

Take, for example, the narrative applied to people with (especially undiagnosed) ADHD all the time – "oh, just focus and you'd be brilliant." Folks apply their own narrative to somebody who has different neurochemistry to them, and grow frustrated when this person can't fit that structure.

But back to Music. Both the film and the character.

One thing this film does is that it has these music videos that take place within Music's head. Now, I've seen people dislike these on principle, but I'm not opposed to the concept – these could (at least in theory) show that just because she struggles to communicate doesn't mean she isn't aware of the world around her, and she's more than a difficulty to others. Except these music videos are a nightmare of harsh colours and flickering lights. This is unpleasant to anybody who has quite a range of sensory issues (which includes a lot of autistic people, as I'm sure you can imagine). Now, combined with how Music dances in the videos (again, since her actress is a talented dancer), and I think that the impression is that, in her own head, Music isn't autistic. That, deep inside, she's "normal".

"Why is this a problem?" You might ask. "If it helps people empathise with what this autistic character is feeling then it's just a useful creative tool."

Narratives, my hypothetical friend (or enemy). Narratives are why this is such an issue. Sure, the film at least gives Music some scraps of character – it's certainly better than the British play All In A Row, where the autistic child is represented by a nightmarish dead-looking puppet who does nothing but scuttle about the stage and meltdown whenever they need a scene transition. But that isn't saying much, is it?

See, the charity called Autism Speaks was involved with this movie (at least in the promotion and distribution). This particular American charity has a well-deserved reputation for their name being a hideous irony – not least because of how they've only ever had one autistic person on their board, and he resigned in protest because they never listened to him. This group seeks to "cure" autism, and promotes "therapies" that purport to "reduce" autism/autistic "symptoms" through downright evil methods of restraint and similar.

Why could someone do this with a clear conscience? Well, when you believe in the narrative of someone being "normal" inside, reducing autistic self-expression would be the same thing as "fixing" parts of them, since you'd believe (and often convince the autistic person themselves) that they are the same inside – so if you stop the external "symptoms" then you've fixed the problem. Statistics about the long-term mental health of people who undergo these sorts of "therapies" tell a compelling story of their own, honestly. Because there's a thing called masking, and most autistic people do it around others and/or in public. But that takes energy and mental effort, and the burnout it can cause is especially bad when you genuinely believe you shouldn't be feeling that way.

Further examples of this narrative include an advert that Autism Speaks once put out called "I am Autism". In this, they cast autism as some kind of malevolent demon – a deep-voiced monster who delights in talking about how he makes marriages fail and incurs debt in families. Narratives like this seem to equate autism with an infectious disease, which I guess helps to set up the idea of "curing" it and revealing the "normal child" inside. (It's always children with these sorts of organisations, they rarely care about the adults.) I think that when you believe that there's some "normal" person trapped inside an autistic shell, and you focus your efforts on that imaginary being, you gradually stop caring about the real person in front of you.

So how does any of this relate to how I started this little ramble? How would "Nothing about us without us" relate to any of this?

Well, as I said, a slogan doesn't explain everything. Now, I hope what I've written has shown a little glimpse of the harmful narratives that ooze out when you cut into the brightly-coloured, feel-good nature of *Music*. I doubt Sia wanted to make something to offend people, since she seems to want to be praised for her work. She's also claimed to have done 3 years of research for this movie, yet fell into all these well-worn and foul old narratives. So imagine this instead – what if, instead of getting her favourite dancer to watch meltdown videos on YouTube to prepare for the role, she got Maddie to talk to autistic people? What if she'd chatted with autistic folks from the start and got their honest feedback about her film? What if she changed things in response to people's well-intentioned criticism instead of blowing up on Twitter? If so, I can't help but imagine the film would have been a lot more respectful, a lot more interesting and might have even, in some small way, actually made the world a better place.

Nothing about us without us.

Hilli Thompson

There Be Dragons

The dragon is a fearsome fiery beast that has marauded in Suffolk. According to the painting in St. Mary's church Wissington, a dragon terrorised the local peasants for years. The painting was completed in roughly 1300, and the legend of the dragon was probably related to another contemporary event.

When Richard 1st returned from his crusade to Jerusalem he returned with a large menagerie which eventually took up residence in the Tower of London. One of the beasts was a very small crocodile. But as it grew and grew and grew, it became mightily distressed by its restrictive environment. In a fit of rage, it burst open its cage and jumped into the River Thames. It swam past Tilbury and the Isle of Dogs and out to sea. It was a fresh water crocodile so it was even crosser in the sea.

And it swam off to sea, up the coast and being very hungry ate a few peasants on the way. Gradually the current took it into the River Stour where it ate many tasty merry peasants. Soon it drifted to Wissington. The local Knights worried about the loss of their workforce ,put on their quivers full of sharpened arrows. But the arrows bounced off the crocodile's armour plating. The crocodile tired of the game thinking that, whilst the locals were tasty they were not friendly, so it swam away.

It was never seen again but it was commemorated in St. Mary's church

Dragons are a universal symbol of good fortune and they turn up in every culture. Often winged it represents both earth and sky - being part eagle and part serpent. It is often seen as a test of strength by virile young men keen on rescuing maidens. The dragon usually holds a sphere in one claw. The sphere is a pearl of wisdom, which the dragon protects.

Dragons come in many guises: beware there may be one near you.

House

On entering the house, one was welcomed by warmth, fragrance and gentle music: someone was making orange marmalade.

From the door, the carpet snaked along the hall and up the stairs in a bright shout of turquoise. Many prints and paintings paraded above the turquoise.

On the landfill windowsill stood a small Cycladic lady, half buried under a begonia and a vase of orange Chinese lanterns.

At the end of the turquoise lay a carmine red and royal blue prayer mat. Over the threshold into the music room stood a harp.

The window was partially coated by a Buddhist hanging; next to it a Buddha smiled.

The gentle music first heard earlier came from a Bass Recorder - an instrument with a rich mellow velvet sound.

Turquoise is symbol of tranquility, the carpet led up to the Buddha's smile and the gently smoothing tones of the recorder. The fragrance of orange marmalade infused.

Orange and turquoise are complementary colours.

March

coming in like a lion

roaring gales, rain, hail

brief glimpses of golden sunshine

reflect yellow daffodils and dandelions

gardens bloom primroses and wallflowers

as brown branches settle

striped tits seek caterpillars in lilac

pigeons coo blackbirds warble

the lion departs like a baaing lamb

Ankita Aggarwal

Merging Into Ecstasy

Ever since she opened her eyes, the little crow bird Nancy knew she wanted to be in the business of flying. She dreamed of being a famous navigator one day and would often argue with her feathery friends why they never aspired for something big in their life.

Nancy even brought her parents onboard with the idea and joined the pioneer flying school where she could learn all the nuances of being the best pilot in the world. She was fascinated by awe-inspiring aircraft and dreamed of having her own someday.

Soon after the initial period of gusto, she started realising how tough it was to be a professional pilot. The incessant lectures and technicalities started giving her the jitters, so much so that her heart would start racing with anxiety as soon as she would enter a flight simulator.

She could not bear it anymore and decided to quit: just then, she heard a faint laughter. As she stepped outside in curiosity, Nancy saw a small group of children playing with their dazzlingly bright kite. She looked at them in amazement as they celebrated the flight of their precious possession claiming a piece of glory of its own.

Nancy crow was struck by the innocence and pleasure of it all. It didn't take her long before she knew she wanted to fly kites! She would have them in all colours, big, small, of different shapes and designs, adorning the sky with all their beauty. And that's what she did. She sourced a huge number of them. Everyday she would have a gala time at the beach along with her soaring kites. It was all fun, simple and uncomplicated. But as the days passed by, she started getting bored of the affair with her kites. There was no more excitement, no more charm. She felt cheated and started questioning the purpose of life.

One day, in sheer frustration, she threw them all away and, finding herself in a pool of tears, she asked herself what is wrong with me?! Why could she not find any contentment? Why had her dreams evaded her? She wanted to run away from this prison of helplessness and fly away from the agony of being a failure.

And suddenly, it struck her. That's what she was supposed to do - FLY! How could she not see it before?

After a moment of hesitation, she took a deep breath of courage, stretched her wings of imagination and took the flight of her dreams until she could lose herself completely and merge with pure ecstasy into the folds of the heavenly skies.

Glimpses of Infinity

The River could feel its death approaching slowly but surely. In its long life, it had travelled through myriad geographies and seen enough of life. It had met the fertile soils of the forest, went through caverns and slopes of the mountains, had the adventures of the waterfall, crossed a vibrant village, gave a little something to a tree, seen the glory of rainbow colours, bowed at the feet of a shrine, laughed and cheered with the Games, cried with the rocks who could never move, giggled with the children enjoying a dip, fumed with anger at Sun's haughtiness, kissed goodbye to the tributaries on its way, raced with the clouds, heard horror tales from the neglected sands, enjoyed fragrances of the orchid, felt the joy of animals, danced with the air and even mourned with the swamp.

Now it was nothing more than a bundle of lifetime memories that she carried with her as she waited for her life to come to an end. The River had always heard the glories of the Ocean, often breathing patiently for its eventuality. Yet the fear of the unknown plagued her. Would she be able to let go? Would she matter within the infinite horizons of the sea? Had she lived enough as a river?

I saw her just as she made her final plunge and merged with the supreme. I never understood what infinity could feel like. I try, seeing its glimpses through the windows of my house and the depths of my heart.

Be The Light – A Folktale

Once upon a time,
In a far away city
Dark clouds wouldn't go away,
Oh such a pity!

There was no sunshine,
Not a good cheer
Sorrow pervaded,
Darkness everywhere!

A child asked his 'fly' friend,
What should be done
Till when they could live,
Without the sun?

The fly saw the tears,
In the child's eyes
And decided to do something,
Consulting other flies.

They all took a tour,
To gauge the situation
And reached the consensus,
Only one thing could be done!

For when it is dark,
With nothing in sight
Take it upon yourself,
To be the source of light!

It would take lots of effort,
Self-transformation too
But given the situation,
It was best for them to do!

They decided to persevere,
Steady and slow
And with strength and focus,
They all began to glow!

The flies became fireflies,
In the city far away
Together they shone,
Till the darkness faded away!

Happiness returned,
With the power divine
Even when it's dark,
There's always a way to shine!

Exploring New Horizons

Thoughts on Well-being and Creative Writing

At Inside Out Community we believe passionately that participation in the arts, discovering and finding an expression for our creativity, can help improve and sustain well-being.

Well-being as a concept is hard to pin down, yet all of us know what it means experientially. It is something to do with how we feel about ourselves and our lives; it is a positive state of health, not simply the absence of ill health; it's about feeling more vibrantly alive; it is something about feeling in balance, in harmony. Well-being is to be found in meeting our needs as human beings – at least partially – within the different dimensions of our lives: the social, psychological, physical, sexual, spiritual and the ecological.

Well-being is not the equivalent of happiness, which is a transient feeling – bursting like sunlight through cloud cover on dull day and disappearing just as quickly. Life is suffering as the Buddha taught; a more sustained sense of well-being comes from living 'right minded lives', a way of being which minimises our own suffering and the suffering of others and helps us accept and transcend it.

Well-being is an underlying feeling of being comfortable with who we are, how we engage with life; something to do with our unfolding as individuals and human beings – being all that we can be and that includes our creative potential. But for others it has less to do with our unfolding individuality and more to do with our social connection and integration.

You can begin to see that well-being is complex. Yet it is a quest that motivates us all – we all seek to move from disharmony to harmony, disequilibrium to equilibrium, from bud to flower. We all know, at some level of awareness, whether our way of being in the world, the circumstances of our lives, is sustaining our well-being. If you had to quantify your well-being over the past month on a continuum – where ten (10) is an enveloping sense of aliveness and grounded positivity, and zero (0) is a kind of persistent, profound dispiritedness and malaise – how would you rate it? If you were to do this simple check-in on your well-being regularly you would discover how sustained (or fluctuating) it is in leaning towards one end of the continuum or the other and you would become more conscious of the determining influences.

So how can writing creatively, if we make it an important part of our lives, contribute to a stronger sense of well-being? It works for me in that I write what I feel most passionately about – what dismays me, what delights me, what captures my interest and imagination; and whether writing in the form of poetry, fiction or creative non-fiction, it gives those experiences substance and truth. However depersonalised and fictionalised my writing is, it always has some resonance for me and my life. It always contains some significant learning, something I need to know or acknowledge. It opens my awareness to new horizons and there is often a profound pleasure in that. If I've spent a few hours writing I often – not always – feel freer, looser, as if I am more in touch with myself somehow.

Poetry (prose writing too) is a kind of container into which we can put our experience of the challenges of life and make some sense of what it means to be human. In that way writing can help us unscramble confusions and draw the sting from the existential anxieties of life. At the very least it offers us a diversion, a refuge from the sometimes overwhelming perplexities and pressures of life; writing can take us to another place, another time.

One of my favourite poets, Emily Dickenson, writes about the power of the imagination to illuminate and enrich our lives. She once wrote; *the brain is wider than the sky / for put them side by side / the one the other will include / with ease and you beside.*[1] While she lived much of her adult life as a recluse, perhaps because of phobic anxiety, she was far from being a prisoner of her anxieties. Her imagination roamed far and wide, and her imaginings are sprinkled liberally throughout her wonderful poetry. The soul should always stand ajar, she said, ready to welcome the ecstatic experience. For Emily, the mere sense of living was enough to find the ecstasy in life. To be a poet – not necessarily a published poet, she was not published in her lifetime – is to connect with the energy of life, to feel its rush, to notice, to be astonished and to find the words to hold to the heart of that experience. To do so gives prominence to 'every now', and 'every now' added together equals our lifetime. Her poetry calls to us not to get lost in the dross of life which robs it of beauty and of meaning.

Susie Orbach, the psychotherapist and writer, suggests that the talking/listening cure is not dissimilar to what happens when one is writing. '*Writing takes us places we had not anticipated and sometimes shocks us with its new un-thought knowledge. This is why many of us write. We want to find out what we didn't know we were thinking and feeling. We want to give shape to inchoate thoughts that need gathering and sorting. The exhilaration of new ideas... or a different emphasis or perspective is what can relieve the hard work of putting new words on the page. It is often this refashioning that subtly resituates us inside ourselves*'.[2]

Rachel Cusk, the novelist, suggests that the desire to write is a desire to live '*more honestly through language*'... '*to assert the true self*'. She argues that '*simplistic as it sounds, finding your true voice is a therapeutic necessity and for many people a matter of urgency. Life offers too few opportunities for self expression and for many people there is too great a disjuncture between how things seem and how they actually feel*'.[3]

The poet Holly McNish talking about the importance of writing in her own life and particularly during the pandemic describes how writing – '*is a distraction and a focus in one*'. She goes on to say – '*Most of the poems I write are primarily for myself: to ease the pain; to heal; to reorganise anger; to giggle; to think more clearly; to acknowledge feelings; to have fun; to play with language; to imagine alternative realities; to wallow; to question; to reconsider; to remember; to give some shape to things that overwhelm me*'.[4]

What has creative writing, in fact any of the arts, to say in times of extremis, such as the current pandemic and the gathering climate crisis? Are the arts at such times irrelevant or a luxury? Peter Reason in his deep reflection 'On Presence' argues that they have a place in grieving for what is lost and in the imaginings of new human possibilities.[5] We need new stories for our time. It is the dominant narratives that change beliefs and our way of being in the world; these may come to us in the stories or poetry we read or listen to; they come to us from what is gestating in our own imaginations and is given life on the page. Think of the wonderful poem by Amanda Gorman performed at the President Biden's inauguration – The Hill We Climb – it is this kind of narrative that changes us: '*if we are only brave enough to see it / if only we are brave enough to be it*'.[6] It is a question for us all to ponder: can we be the future we want to see; want to live?

We use the term 'humanity' to signify what is best in humankind – a compassionate, benevolent and loving way of being; and my contention is that the personal resonances of a poem and other forms of creative fiction and non fiction can help connect us with what is deepest in ourselves – what is 'real' and essentially 'good'.

Inside Out Community warmly invites you to join the

Write Minds programme and explore how making creative writing part of your life can work for you to help sustain and improve well-being. For more information go to www.insideoutcommunity.com.

Peter Watkins (2021)
Co-Founder
Inside Out Community

---

[1] Emily Dickenson's poem 623, The Brain is Wider Than the Sky, is widely available in collections and on-line. It continues: *The Brain is Deeper Than the Sea...* And ends: *The Brain is Just the Weight of God...* It is a poem about our capacity for imagination.

[2] Orbach S. (2016) The Poetry of Therapy. Guardian Newspaper. October 29th

[3] Cusk R. (2013) In Praise of the Creative Writing Course. Guardian Newspaper. January 18th

[4] McNish (2021) In - The View From the Here. Guardian Newspaper. Review May 18th

[5] Reason P, Gillespie S. (2019) On Presence. The Letter Press, Exeter.

[6] Gorman A. (2021) The Hill We Climb. Chatto & Windus, London.

All the contributing authors were posed the question:
"Why do you write?"
This Word Cloud was created from their answers

Appendices

Contributing Authors

Brendan Wilson
I grew up in the 1970s, a time when, perhaps even more than now, people had to hide their mental health difficulties and mine became apparent from quite a young age. I have found that creativity is very helpful. Initially I worked as a photographer and filmmaker and I have found that with writing it is also useful to be a natural observer. Given that I am not neuro typical I write from the perspective of the outsider. Mental health is often viewed negatively but from the inside of the experience, it seems that judgements of happiness are subjective, idiosyncratic and often prejudiced. People often feel that because someone has a mental health problem that their lives are unhappy ones. This is not the case. I try to write positively and honestly about people and situations that would often not be viewed positively. Song writing, anything from Stevie Wonder to John Spillane, influences me as much as other writing and occasionally a lyric will, in one form or another, find its way into my writing.

Jan Addison
I have not always succeeded, but paying attention to, and finding an expression for, the attributes which make up the acronym of creativity (see below) has been essential to my mental health and physical welfare, particularly since we were plunged into the a strange and surreal world that we have inhibited for the past fifteen months. Much of this expression can take place in the process of living creatively.

C – Curiosity
R – Resilience
E – Energy
A – Attention
T – Trust
I – Instinct
V– Versatility
I – Insight
T –Thoughtfulness
Y –Yearning

Caroline Izzard
Expressing my creativity is a means of navigating the sometimes turbulent waters of the recovery process. Writing and art awards me the freedom to share my ideas and experiences, and my own unique interpretation of the world in a safe and non-threatening way. The focus and absorption help to calm the soul and steady the ship, providing a direction and sense of purpose. I am on an exciting journey of discovery which is ongoing – there is always more to learn and explore!

Simon Black
I find writing an incredibly rewarding experience and I feel very privileged when I can share it with anyone. Writing is a way of exploring yourself. You can be anyone, or anything, you want to be when you are writing, and as T. S. Eliot says,

"*We shall not cease from exploration*
And the end of all our exploring
Will be to arrive where we started
And know the place for the first time."

I find returning to myself after writing very refreshing. I once lived abroad, came back to the UK after a few years, and saw my home town for the first time. Seeing something for the first time is observing with fresh eyes the wonder that it is, even though we've seen it many times before. Writing for me is exactly that.

Alan Vickers
I had never done any creative writing before joining the Write Minds courses, but now I can't imagine not writing. It's a revelation when the penny drops and you realise that fiction authors have complete freedom to invent any characters, in any locations, in any situations, following any plot that you care to dream up for them. I've come to value creative fiction writing as a liberating, positively addictive, and ultimately satisfying hobby that has provided such a positive impact to my life. Thanks to Inside Out Community and Write Minds, I have developed a fondness for writing self-contained short stories. I've now written over 30 of them, ranging from 100-word micro-fictions to 10,000-word fully-fledged short stories. None of these would have existed if I'd not discovered Write Minds. Even though they may never go anywhere else, I have loved the experience of creating them for myself out of thin air.

Tess Last
My name is Tess Last, I'm a 50-something living in Ipswich with 3 cats, a husband, and bipolar disorder. I write (mainly poetry) crochet, draw, paint, and doodle. Creativity is vital to me as it's an outlet in the dark times and an expression of joy in the calm times. Here is what Write Minds means to me:

W*ords wonderfully powerful*
R*ecording of fiction and fact*
I*nventive ways to communicate*
T*ouching the heart of creativity*
E*xpression of possibilities*

M*ind melding imagination*
I*nspirational exploration*
N*on-judgemental mixing of ideas*
D*ivinely inventive*
S*upportive nurturing creation*

Kenny Mackay
I started writing four or five years ago as I was keen to write a piece of memoir. It became obvious to me that I needed to learn how to write - so I joined Write Minds sessions. Writing quickly became a total absorption for me in a way I couldn't have imagined. Incredibly enriching and satisfying - if not sometimes challenging! I write because it can also be lots of fun and deeply rewarding - helping me get to know myself and process life.

Mick Grant
I don't know why I write. Mostly I write songs. Some of them became a rock opera. I've written a short novel, and my latest work is a rock musical about a woman that dies early and is sent back to her boyfriend in another woman's body. I call it a supernatural romantic black comedy. An idea comes, and I get on with it. Folk ask me if it's 'cathartic'. It isn't, even though it comes from my own life. Writing sometimes makes me live

the feelings again. It's not an expression of myself, not a hobby, not any of the reasons other folk say they write. I do like it, though.

Diane Pilbro
I write for enjoyment; inspired by nature and natural phenomena. Forests offer me solace to write and think. I've interest in music, creativity and the drum. I write to the rhythm of the music. The white noise I create, helps me to focus on the task I am doing. Also, interest in travel; culture, the vast languages and dialects of the world. Pleasure in exploring words and rhythm of language. Expressing emotion; bringing prose to life. Exploring ideas, giving them meaning and form. Encapsulating thoughts in a cognitively provocative manner, evincing avidity. Non resonating fervour resolved by architectural manuscript. Conceptions realised; any conundrum solved.

Brendan Pearson (1952 - 2020)
Brendan was a gentle, beautiful, intelligent man who struggled with searing anxieties throughout most of his adult life. He was a true creative who found satisfaction and consolation in the expression for his creative energies in music, singing, drama, poetry, and creative writing. For several years he served as a trustee of Inside Out Community.

Mai Black
Poetry helps me appreciate the world around me and gain a sense of balance, and all that experience - whether positive or negative - is of equal benefit when writing a poem. Currently I'm working as a Creative Mentor for Inside Out Community; leading workshops for Suffolk Writers Group; and am in the final stages of publishing a collection of poems - each written in the voice of a famous historical character. It's called '*30 Angry Ghosts: Poems for Performance*' and it should be available on Amazon from August 2021.

Sallyanne Webb
Why I write.
For me, the blank paper is my therapist, my confidante, my muse, my healer, my playmate, my challenger, my admirer, my anchor, my light, my hope.

Peter Watkins
For me, writing, particularly poetry, is a way of celebrating being alive. It sometimes takes me on a descent into dark places but always returns me to the light. Creativity is at the hub of my life - as expression, as exploration, as healing.

Maggie Singleton
I am no longer young.
I write for myself, without seeking praise or judgement; to express feelings without perhaps attributing them; to describe my world to those that do not share it. And yes, to ease the heartache that sometimes threatens to shatter me.

Esme Pears
I write and make art because I don't know any other way to be. For me, both are methods of exploration - into the world and myself - and as such enable me to move deeper into my life and to connect more meaningfully with others while retaining a sense of not-knowing.

Thomas Freestone
Hello there, I'm Thomas – currently working as a laboratory technician. I started writing with Write Minds in Autumn 2019, quite some time before I got this job. Creativity (and creative writing in particular) has been a lifeline throughout the last four years, firstly helping to pull me out of some bad mental places and then keeping me at an equilibrium whilst I hunted for jobs after university. Writing, for me, is about communication. As an autistic person, there's often a lot to worry about in day-to-day conversations – I like to think I'm getting better at picking up nuances, but I'm nowhere near

perfect, especially if I'm stressed or excited! Creative writing for me is like a conversation with my reader, but one where I can control the pace and flow, without fear of stepping on toes.

Hilli Thompson
B.A.hons/MPhil Anthropology P.G.C.E (Mental Handicap). Taught severely disabled children for 4 years. Left to work as professional visual artist, which continues to today. Worked with wide range of people including Parkinson's patients. Worked with day-care patients in St. Elizabeth's Hospice and still working there for one shift a week. Trained Buddhist chaplain. Musician and gardener.
Creative work reflects my quirky soul.

Ankita Aggarwal
Inside Out Community has given me an opportunity to look deep within and have the confidence to write. The thoughts when meshed up in my mind are irrelevant and of little value until I write them down on paper. Words give me comfort of that little space carved out just for me, where I am safe and at home. It is an icing on the cake when others are able to relate with it too. For this, I would like to thank Inside Out Community in a poem:

Thank You INSIDE OUT COMMUNITY
To thank the rains, the tree GROWS
To thank the air, life FLOWS
To thank the sun, the earth DANCES
To thank the fire, smoke RISES
To thank the earth, nature REJOICES
I hope I can, someday, do all those things
To be able to truly say my thanks to you!

Photography Credits

Page	Photo
Cover	*Green Wind sculpture* - **Alan Vickers**
vi	*Black River & Haiku* - **Brendan Wilson**
4	*Silver Birch & Haiku* - **Brendan Wilson**
12	Pixabay.com stock - MabelAmber
14, 16, 17	*Caroline's Junk Journal* - **Caroline Izzard**
19-27	*Come Out, Hedgehog! picture book* - **Caroline Izzard**
30	*Sleeping Baby & Haiku* - **Brendan Wilson**
34	Pexels.com stock- Ketut Subiyanto
49	*Poppy* - **Alan Vickers**
52	Unsplash.com stock - Emmersen Doane
54	Unsplash.com stock - Zdeněk Macháče
60	Unsplash.com stock - Jon Tyson
74	*Snow & Haiku* - **Brendan Wilson**
82	Unsplash.com stock - Callum Skelton
88	*Algae & Haiku* - **Brendan Wilson**
92	*Tree of Life & Haiku* - **Brendan Wilson**
96	*Crocus & Haiku* - **Brendan Wilson**
102	*Just a Day & Haiku* - **Brendan Wilson**
108	Unsplash.com stock - Richard Lee
114	Unsplash.com stock - Mehdi Sepehri
122	*Kyson* - **Alan Vickers**
126	Unsplash.com stock - Keerthivasan Swaminathan
132	*Impression* - **Alan Vickers**
138	*Word Cloud* - **Alan Vickers**